I0741917

First Came Fear

First Came Fear

edited by
Casey Ellis

Also in the NEW series

Southern Gothic: New Tales of The South edited by Brian Centrone &
     Jordan M. Scoggins
Behind the Yellow Wallpaper: New Tales of Madness edited by Rose Yndigoyen
Startling Sci-Fi: New Tales of the Beyond edited by Casey Ellis

Other titles by New Lit Salon Press

I Voted for Biddy Schumacher: Mismatched Tales from the Mind of Brian Centrone
Erotica by Brian Centrone
Salon Style: Fiction, Poetry & Art edited by Brian Centrone

First Came Fear: New Tales of Horror

Published by New Lit Salon Press, 2018

© 2018 New Lit Salon Press, LLC

Edited by Casey Ellis
Editor-in-Chief, Brian Centrone
Line Edited by Rose Yndigoyen
Art by Luke Spooner
Art Direction and Design by luke kurtis

"Loved to Death" was previously published at *FootstepsofGhosts.com* in 2009,
Wattpad.com in 2010, and *QuarterReads.com* in 2015.

All rights reserved. No part of this book may be used or reproduced by any means,
graphic, electronic, or mechanical, including photocopying, recording, taping or
by any information storage retrieval system without the written permission of the
publisher except in the case of brief quotations embodied in critical articles and
reviews.

This collection of stories is a work of fiction. All characters are fictionalized. Any
resemblance to those living or dead is purely coincidental.

New Lit Salon Press
Carmel, NY

Print ISBN 978-0-9972649-2-0

www.newlitsalonpress.com

Table of Contents

A Logical Explanation

Ken Teutsch

J ulian laughed suddenly and pointed.

"Looks just like the poster!"

The reflection of the dark mass of the tree line and that of the setting sun behind it were smeared across the surface of the old man's pond. Everything not black was splashed with blood-red. The frogs and insects were raising a raucous noise. Fireflies blinked just above the tops of the weeds at the water's edge. The place had looked pretty dumpy in the afternoon light, but now…

"See what I mean?" he said.

"Do what?" said the old man. He had been quiet since following Julian out of the house, though he had certainly been talkative enough before. Julian had to be almost rude to tear himself away.

"It's just that…" Julian swept an arm across to indicate the scene. "This looks just like the poster. The movie poster!" He reached into his pocket for his phone. He wanted to get a picture before the light disappeared, and it was fading quickly. "*The Legend of Boggy Creek*. You know, it has that great poster with the Creature running through the water in silhouette against—"

"Didn't care for that movie," the old man said, and spat. "Seen it on TV. Didn't care for it."

"Yeah," said Julian. *No shit!* he added to himself. The old man had made that very clear in the course of their talk. Pretty much the whole conversation had been a downer, with the old guy scoffing at reported Fouke Monster sightings, throwing out some pretty choice words about his neighbors' credibility, reliability and common sense in the process. He didn't care much for his neighbors' creature stories, but he really, *really* didn't like that movie. He kept tediously coming back to it until Julian was vindictively tempted to tell the old guy about all the lousy sequels.

Nearly everyone else Julian had approached around Fouke, Arkansas

over his three days canvassing the area had enthusiastically endorsed the existence of a large, bipedal cryptid in the area. Not that the Jethros used those terms. (When he talked to his pals back home, Julian's designation for the local was either "Jethro" or "Ellie Mae." He switched from TV to the movies when referring to the kids: them he called, "Dueling Banjos.") Everybody—all ages—loved to talk about the mysterious creature, and many said they'd seen it themselves. Literally everybody knew someone who had seen it…or run from it…or shot at it. But this old guy—he was too old to be a Jethro…this "Jed"—was a real wet blanket on the subject. He didn't exactly say the creature didn't exist, just that his neighbors were all full of shit.

Well, anyway. At least he had figured out he couldn't use the geezer before wasting time setting up his video camera.

"You gonna make another movie?" said the old man. His voice was low.

"A documentary," Julian said. *Like I told you, Jed.* "For the web, but we're hoping to get streaming distribution. You know. Netflix, maybe." Had this guy even heard of Netflix? Or the internet, for that matter? Julian tilted his phone this way and that, but the "poster moment" was gone. The red was darkening with surprising speed. He put the phone away. "Well, I'd better be going. Thanks for your time."

He turned, and took a startled step back. The old man was standing very close.

"You folks," he said, his face downturned and shadowed, "with your movies and your TV shows and your books…" There was something odd about his voice now. It hadn't been so low before. He sounded hoarse. Julian took another step back, his heel sinking into the damp soil near the water. To his amazement, he began to feel hairs actually rising on the back of his neck.

"Ya'll get it all wrong." There was a tinge of regret in the now strangely gravelly voice. "All

wrong."

What light was left had completely lost its redness. The old man's t-shirt, what was visible above his overalls, seemed to float in the murk. His white hair was a glowing smudge in the darkness. Julian found that he had to swallow before he could speak.

"Oh?" he said. "But you… You know what's really going on?"

The old man's head jerked up and Julian twitched back involuntarily. A green eye glinted with its own light. "Yes, sir," said the old man. "I do. I surely do."

"Yeah. O.K." Julian side-stepped around him. His car was under the oak tree in the front yard. It seemed so far away now, lost in the shadows. *Jesus Christ, it gets dark fast around here!*

"I'm sure you're right," Julian called back over his shoulder. "Sure, there's a logical explanation." He began to walk faster. "Better be going now. Thanks!" The old man didn't reply, but Julian thought he heard a raspy sound of in-drawn breath. Julian couldn't see his car in the tree's shadow, but he could see the tree, lit by a white light, dim but growing. He could hear his footfalls now, suddenly loud, thumping in the grass. Why did his footsteps suddenly sound so…

The night noises had stopped. The crickets or whatever they were… the frogs. They were silent. Everything was silent. He could hear his own shallow breathing.

I'm panicking! Why am I panicking? What's going on?

Julian heard a cough behind him, loud, low and wet. Not a sound an old man—or any man—would make. Then he heard a growl, and he stopped wondering and started running.

The last thing he saw was the full moon above the eastern tree line.

Loved to Death

Michael J.P. Whitmer

Family and friends had gathered under a large canopy tent to attend the graveside service for Jonathan Hill's mother. The pastor conducting the service read from John 14:27.

"Let not your heart be troubled…" His words trailed off, leaving him staring toward the back of the tent.

"Can I help you?" The pastor asked a doctor, standing just at the edge of the tent, garbed in his surgical scrubs from head to toe.

Those in attendance, including Jon and his father, who sat at the front nearest to the open casket, turned to look down the aisle at the sudden arrival.

"I would like to say a few words," the doctor stated, making his way down the walkway toward the front of the gathering. Stopping at the casket, he positioned himself behind it, facing the family.

"I'm so sorry…there wasn't anything more I could do…" he said, shaking his head from side to side. Reaching into the casket, the doctor slowly pulled from it a slimy, bloody, screaming newborn baby girl. He held it toward Jon and his father.

"I'm sorry!"

Jon shot upright from the couch. His breathing was deep and beads of sweat dotted his forehead. The same nightmare had been plaguing his sleep ever since the move.

"Change is healthy. It'll help to start somewhere new, somewhere to make new memories," he remembered his father telling him.

Help who? He wished he had asked him then.

It was hard enough for a fifteen-year-old to cope with the loss of his mother seven months ago, but to ask him to up and move, leaving behind everything he'd ever known?

That was too much, Jon thought.

Jon knew better, though. He knew the move was more for his father, who had been looking for a way out long before his mother's death. He could still hear their late-night fighting in his head. His father going on about how this wasn't the life he wanted, and his mother calling him a coward, among other things. No matter what was thrown or screamed his mom would always come into his room after the situation had settled. Sometimes her eyes were red from crying or her voice hoarse from yelling, but she assured him every time: "We'll always be a family," and would seal it with a kiss.

There was a boom of thunder and a flash of lightning that sent Jon jumping out of thought. The storm had been raging all night and showed no sign of letting up. From upstairs, he could make out his baby sister, Melissa, crying.

Jon looked at the clock on the wall.

Nine-seventeen. Dad should be home soon, he reminded himself, thankfully. Like most teens, he despised babysitting.

Springing off the sofa, Jon headed to the staircase near the foyer. Reluctantly, he began to ascend the stairs, and with every step he took, his sister's crying became more and more audible over the unwavering storm outside. Reaching the second floor, the lights cut off freezing him where he was, flickering back to life a moment later. Breathing easier, Jon continued into the hall towards his sister's room.

Standing at Melissa's door, her shrieking became even worse. Jon reached for the knob.

"What the…" he wondered puzzled as to why the door wouldn't open.

Trying the knob the other way and then both ways again but with a bit more force, it still didn't budge. The door was locked.

But how?

The lights cut out once more without powering back on. In the pitch-black things seemed heightened, silence twice as quiet and the slightest of noises amplified. His sister's crying was no exception, going from ear-throbbing to ear-piercing. Jon had to get to her for her sake and his sanity's.

The window! The thought crossed his mind.

There was a trellis under the window that he could climb from the backyard.

Pushing through the dark, he cautiously made his way back down stairs, away from the maddening, dominating sounds of his sister's constant crying, where the storm's rage ruled. Through the living room,

Jon followed along the wall and into the kitchen, fumbling his way to the rear door that led to the backyard. Jon opened it to a strong blast of wind that swept the door from his grasp, slamming it against the wall. Wind and rain rushed inside in frenzy, sending Jon in a panic to get the door closed, which he finally did, leaning his weight against it.

"Maybe I'll just wait for Dad to get home," he thought, second-guessing his adolescent plan.

As if Melissa had read his mind, her screams seemed to erupt tenfold, batting back his most recent idea.

Jon huffed, shaking his head in frustration at what he was about to do. Opening the backdoor once more, bracing it to hold the weather at bay; he stood behind it like a shield, peering out into the night. The storm was relentless: wild winds tossing the rain madly at all angles.

Frowning, he braved the storm where he was instantly drenched. Moving across the porch, Jon squinted attempting to look through the night and rain. He ran off the patio and onto the flooded grass until he stopped under Melissa's window. Leaping onto the trellis, he scaled it as quickly as possible. Pulling his top half up to look into the glass, there was nothing but blackness and his reflection staring back at him. As he moved to open the window from the bottom, his own reflection faded into a pale woman's—his mother's. Jon gasped and went falling from the ledge. With a heavy thud, he hit the wet ground head and back first.

He moaned, sloshing in the wet grass, as he slowly crawled to his feet. With a throbbing head, Jon could barely stand. Stumbling hazily through the yard and rain-turned-drizzle, Jon managed to find his way into the house.

Jon's eyes blinked open. He was lying on the couch, completely soaked, with a terrible headache.

How? He wondered as he sat up, noticing the lights were back on.

The teen remembered making a try for the window and slipping off the trellis.

"But how did I get back in…?"

His sister's screams interrupted the thought. It had gotten to the point where he wanted to scream back at her, tell her to shut up. Instead, he took a deep breath. Rolling off the couch, he marched towards the stairs.

Jon meant to get into Melissa's room if he had to kick down the door to do so.

Reaching the foyer, the distinct sound of metal crunching sounded outside, stopping Jon where he stood. It dawned on him, his dad wasn't home yet, and it sent his heart plummeting into his gut, causing a sickening feeling. Frantically, he averted his course towards the front door where he swung it open. The storm had let up, though the boy hadn't noticed, for his eyes were fixed across the street on his father's car wrapped around the foot of a large tree. Jon took off through the doorway, sprinting along the driveway, and straight across the street.

"Dad!" He arrived at the scene.

The car had t-boned the tree on the driver's side. His dad was motionless within the vehicle, and there was a splat of blood where the tree and driver's side window had met.

"Dad!"

Tears brought on by fear had already begun to pool in the corners of his eyes. He scrambled around the car, making his way to the passenger side, and halted. Something caught his eye. Through tears, he looked down to the end of the street—the direction his dad had been coming—there stood a woman in a white hospital gown.

"Mom?"

Jon couldn't breathe; he couldn't speak or move. It felt like an ice cube had melted down the arch of his back, freezing his spine over. The tears now streamed down his cheeks.

There was a crack of lightning that lit the sky, and she was gone, leaving Jon sobbing and powerless to move. He tried to grasp exactly what he had seen, but his mind was a blur of mass confusion and terror. It reached out for one thought. Get help.

"Get help." Jon told himself again.

The thought forced him to move, making a mad dash back to the house.

The teen nearly ran through the door on his way inside. He went for the kitchen where the portable house phone was mounted.

"Nine, one, one," Jon recited the numbers as he punched them in and brought the receiver to his ear.

There was nothing. The lines were down.

On the verge of tears once more is when Jon noticed the silence. It was a stillness he would have welcomed earlier but now dreaded. Listening closely, there was only the faint sound of the storm rolling away in the distance. Melissa's crying had ceased.

The boy placed the phone back on the base and warily began to walk from the kitchen toward the stairs. Gradually, he made his way up to the second floor, pressing through the silence, down the hall, and stopping at Melissa's door that was now eerily ajar. Jon eased it open, stepping into the room. Bit by bit he closed the distance between him and his sister's crib until he was looking into it. Melissa lay unmoving, voiceless, and totally lifeless.

"Oh God." The words rolled weakly from his trembling lips.

From behind Jon, a tranquil humming enveloped him like a cold embrace. It was a familiar woman's voice, one he could have never forgotten. His heart pounded, threatening to erupt from his chest, and each breath became feebler and more unable to appease his lungs.

"Jonny…" The haunting voice whispered, calling to him.

"Jonny…" It welcomed the boy again, urging him to turn and face her.

Jon gulped and slowly turned to the voice—to his mother—sitting in the rocking chair, gently swaying back and forth. Melissa cooed in her arms, and his father stood beside them. Jon's eyes went wide; he was instantly fear stricken, incapable of releasing the scream of horror bottled up in his throat.

"Come see your sister." The ghost smiled.

Jon remained unable to blink or speak. He had begun to inch toward the door, easing himself out of the room in reverse. His eyes never once left the three until he backed out of the room. He hurried through the hall and began to turn to make it down the stairs when the lights cut out. The power flickered on, revealing Jon's mother within kissing distance of his face. He went stumbling before crashing down the steps.

The boy lay dead at the bottom of the staircase, his neck broken from the fall.

"We're a family again…"

Mother-in-Law's Tongue

Daniel Gooding

"**D**o you want to close the blind in the living room?"

As you reach for the cord, one of the tall, green leaves brushes against your wrist; the feeling is cold and clammy, almost nauseating for some reason. The blind shoots down quicker than you expect, catching the rearmost leaves of the plant in its slats and pulling it towards the window. You yank the cord back up again, but this only lifts the plant higher, tilting it forward. You instinctively lunge for it, but in your panic and mistiming you end up punching the saucer base in an uppercut, sending the whole thing tumbling to the floor in a shower of earth and crispy leaf fragments.

"Fuck's sake!"

You bend down to pick up the pot and its saucer, the thick meaty leaves almost pinning it to the ground, and thump it back onto the windowsill. Becky walks in at this point, with perfect timing.

"When are you gonna get rid of some of these fucking plants?"

"Oh, shut up," Becky replies.

"They're just clogging up the windowsill. And every time I shut the blinds they get knocked onto the bloody floor!"

"Move them forward then! Or is that too much of an effort for you?"

"Well, can't we at least cut them back or something?" you reply. "Just shear one side of it perfectly flat so it doesn't get snarled up in the fucking blind all the time?"

"They're good for the atmosphere; they neutralize the traffic fumes from outside."

"Put them outside then. They can suck it all up before it gets through the window."

Becky's response to this is a high-pitched *mi-mi-mi-mi-mi*, to signify your whininess.

"Fine. I'll wait until you go out to work tomorrow and then pitch it out onto the street."

"My mum gave us that plant!"

"She gave *you* the plant Becky, let's be honest—I just happened to be there at the time."

"Oh yes, that's right, because my mum's a total bitch isn't she! Christ, you just can't leave it alone, can you?"

Becky flounces out of the room, slamming the door behind her. A minute later you hear the kitchen tap running, followed by the angry clattering of plates and cups. You stand there paralyzed, ruing your final comment. Pulling your hair up into a gritty peak between your fingers, you stare for a moment at the sulking plant, before going to the hall cupboard to get out the vacuum cleaner.

You only met Becky's mother last year, flying out to Toulouse the previous summer for that very purpose. Whether her condition was a chemical reaction to your sudden appearance in her daughter's life, or a manifestation of her long-standing resentment towards the world, you aren't entirely sure, but by the time you finally made it home from the airport, her voice was already waiting for you on the answerphone with the news that her doctor had just diagnosed her with bowel cancer.

After the long phone call and the seemingly endless tears and recriminations, you told Becky to go to bed, to try and get some rest and let you finish unpacking. Mostly this was so you wouldn't have to endure her constant sniffing and those baleful red eyes. She had just shaken her head though, sitting hunched on the sofa and taking items out of the bag one at a time. Then she'd found the plant amongst your clothes, looking not unlike a human head in its opaque packaging.

The day after your arrival in Toulouse, having driven down to the nearby shopping complex in the scorching heat, Becky's mother had found this large leafy green plant, which she had insisted on buying for you. *S. trifasciata* it said on the label, then in English: "Snake Plant (also known as Saint George's Sword, or Mother-in-Law's Tongue). She had taken much amusement from this last name, drawing your attention to it with a potentially well-meaning grin. Despite Becky's assertion that you would give her the ten euros for it, her mother had insisted to the point of anger that you let her pay for it, claiming repeatedly that it would be something to remind you of her in the flat.

Despite having spent several hours in its plastic cocoon, the plant still seemed as fresh and green as when it had first gone into the bag.

Although it seems silly, you handled the plant tentatively, as though some of her carcinogens might have been transferred into the soil. Normally you would have asked Becky where the best place to stick the plant was, but at this point she had begun to emit a high-pitched keening noise, so you placed it down in the middle of the kitchen table, visible through the doorway as you sat down to give her a hug.

From that day forward, Becky's mother is constantly in your house. Every morning you get up and open the blinds, contending with the plant's cloying leaves, before Becky hurries into the room to check her phone, just in case her mother has been in touch. Come the evening, after a usually long and tedious day, you sink into the sofa as Becky confides her latest fears and apprehensions about her mother, stuck out there all on her own with nobody there for her *should anything happen*; you dumbly pat her for a moment in bemused consolation, before she trudges off to the bathroom, and you get up to carefully lower the blind again.

You arrive home this evening to a muted reception, a sure sign these days of the calm before the inevitable storm, and after a brief exchange of hostilities you lie now on the sofa trying to get to sleep. You shift slightly under the sweaty covers, trying to gauge the time from the alarm clock that blazes a dull red in the corner of the room, when you get the impression that you are no longer alone in the room.

A very faint hissing noise reaches your ear; paralyzed by a sudden pulse of pure fear, you lie there as it traces a sharp claw along your scrotum. Before you can summon the courage to move, you feel a delicate, almost erotic tightening around your neck. You regain your senses just as panic is about to overwhelm you, grabbing and pulling at the thing around your neck. The fleshy strand refuses to tear between your fingers, and you tumble the short distance to the floor, gouging your knee on the corner of something in the process.

You hear the light click on down the corridor as Becky's feet come shuffling in your direction.

"What are you doing?"

The voice is tired and bemused, yet with a hint of unexpected tenderness. It's a tone you haven't heard for a while, but before you can respond in kind the unexpected nature of what has happened takes over.

"That fucking plant just tried to strangle me!"

Becky just stares at you.

"I swear to God, it had its fucking hands around my throat!"

An eyebrow lifts skeptically.

"Alright—hand, leaf, tendril! Whatever the fuck it is, it was trying to kill me!"

Becky sighs.

"You really believe the plant wants to kill you?"

She walks over and peers into your eyes.

"Are you even awake?"

"Yes, I'm not dreaming! I can still feel where the leaves were around my neck. Can you see any red marks?"

You lift your head up to give her a better look at your throat, but she continues to look at you with the same disbelieving frown.

"Why would the plant want to kill you? I know you have this whole ongoing feud with it, but I'd always thought it was more one-sided."

"Who the hell knows? Maybe it's your mother's doing—maybe she's operating it psychically, wrapping her claws round some carved puppet to make it do her evil bidding!"

The sleepiness drops from her eyes instantly. You think about blurting out an apology before she can respond, but at the same time something seems to stop you.

"You're such a dickhead, you know that?"

She turns and stomps off down the corridor.

"Stay out of my way tomorrow," is the last thing you hear before the bedroom door slams shut.

You stand there, decrepit, an erection nuzzling your pajama bottoms at the sight of Becky in her underwear. You look at the plant on the windowsill, utterly motionless now like a spider that knows it's being watched.

Three days later, you are alone in the flat. The night of your second-to-last big argument, Becky's mother had apparently deteriorated quite significantly; more accurately you might say her condition had just dropped suddenly, like a plane hitting an air pocket. She had told Becky over the phone that she was slowly fighting her way back, but she made it sound like a steep uphill struggle, and certainly did nothing to dissuade her from flying out there as soon as she could get the time off work.

You shut the front door behind you as you arrive home from the office, feeling the cool silence and the absence of tension that sweeps through the rooms like a breeze. Without Becky around there is no sense of hostility in the air, no sense of dread on the bus coming home, culminating in the knot in the stomach that tightens as you slot your key into the front door.

You make yourself a cup of tea and put on the television, where one of the various sub-channels is showing *The Fellowship of the Ring* for what must be the third time this week. As you relax into the familiar storyline, you turn and look at the plant on the windowsill, but for some reason you feel no danger from it now. This is not to say that the threat is not still there but, like the eye of Sauron you feel its attention is currently focused elsewhere, a long distance away over untold vistas of murky wastelands.

About an hour later, just as you are about to push yourself up from the sofa to go to the toilet during an ad break, you are startled by a sudden thump, as something lands on the thick carpet. Looking down, you see one of the African sculptures lying on its side where it has fallen from the windowsill, and once again you feel that ball-tightening sensation of impending terror. You look towards the plant, and can see that its tendrils are quivering as though they have recently been shaken. By a sneeze perhaps, or a racking cough. The crispy brown flowers rub gently against the wooden blinds you so despise, making an almost imperceptible sound as of small, rasping breaths.

That infinitesimal noise, and the image it suddenly scratches in your mind's eye, pushes you over the edge. You grab the plant pot, surprised not only by its relative lightness but also the coldness of the terracotta against your skin and, holding it at arms' length, you stride down the long winding corridor and out into the main hallway. The outside window is propped wide open as it generally is during the summer, and below is the small courtyard where the dustbins are kept. Without stopping to look in case anyone is down there, you push the plant out through the gap into thin air. You hear a sharp yet muffled crack from below, and a white light bursts in the enclosed space. The plant lies in the middle of a scattered expanse of soil like a bomb crater; even from this height you can see the leaves still quivering under the spotlights, as if it had been caught trying to make a prison break.

You pull the window closed as far as it will go, and walk back into the flat, putting the catch on as well as sliding the chain across as you do so. After killing the lights in the living room, you go straight into the bedroom and climb under the covers. You see your phone on the bedside table, and feel a sudden urge to call Becky. You dial the number, but it rings and rings before going to voicemail.

Lying back on the pillow, you feel a calmness coming over you now that the plant is out of the house, as if something dreadful has suddenly receded. No doubt Becky will have something to say about it when she comes back, but under the circumstances she has more important things to worry about. You realize you could have just shaken the plant out of its base rather than throwing the pot out as well, or wrenched it out with your bare hands and cast it down. But something had instinctively warned you against touching the plant itself, though you couldn't say what.

You are awake again, but with no recollection of falling asleep. There is a strange green ambience to the room you don't recall being there before, but on turning to your left you see that the light is coming from your phone. You grab it just in time to see an incoming call from Becky before it rings off; immediately you try to call her back, but it goes straight to answerphone, so you wait and try again, but the same thing happens. Either her phone has just died or she is leaving you a very long voice message.

As you lie back, waiting for the message to come through, you feel a sudden chill run through you; not a chill, more a pang of something. At the same time, you picture Becky pacing up and down the hallway of some unnamed French hospital, tears streaming down her face as she shares all her thoughts and fears for her mother with your answerphone, because you're too busy sleeping to listen. Or care. You think about her mother, lying in a clinical green bed amongst caring and uncaring strangers, wracked with pain and worn down by years of bitterness and resentment, the final moments of a long and mostly unhappy life.

Then you think of the plant; the plant given to you as a gift by Becky's mother, the token of thoughtfulness and love from a woman who has learned too late how to impart such things. You think about Becky coming home alone, tired and emotional from saying goodbye to her mum, and finding that same plant broken and withered amongst the rotten food and other refuse; because you hate her mother and wanted to injure her in whatever pathetic, passive-aggressive way you could manage.

You rise out of bed in one fluid motion, without stopping to put on a T-shirt or anything else. You open the front door to the flat, barely noticing the bolt and chain as you release them, and walk quietly down the stairs and out to the courtyard; you wait a moment for the light to spring on again, but nothing happens. Maybe the bulb has gone. Two of the neighbors still seem to be up at this hour though, and in the dim light from their windows you can see the plant where it landed. It doesn't appear to have moved, as though it has been lying there in the hope that you would shortly come back for it.

Slowly you carry it back upstairs and into the kitchen. Unable to see a jug or other receptacle large enough to hold it, you stand there indecisively until an idea comes to you. Filling the basin with cold water you carefully push the plant down into the sink in an attempt to make it stand up, eventually leaning it against the side as a compromise.

There is a noise coming from the bedroom, a faint burring sound. An inch of the old fear comes back to you, but then you realize it must be your phone again. You remember the message that will be waiting for you, but impatient now to speak to Becky you run to the bedroom, once more lit up by the intermittent green glow of the screen.

Tumbling onto the bed, you grab the phone and answer.

"Hello?"

"Hey, it's me."

"Hey, how's it going?"

Becky lets out a long sigh, and for a moment you fear that your question is too insensitive, but you realize that it is a sigh of relief, of someone having overcome an ongoing and difficult obstacle in the road.

"I'm okay. I'm sorry if I woke you."

"No, I was up anyway. Honestly."

As yours eyes accustom to the light, you see that your hands are still caked in soil from carrying the plant, some of which is now smattered over the bed sheets. The strange feelings of tenderness and empathy you experienced a moment ago begin to fade, as you think about the washing you'll have to do before Becky gets back.

"How's things down there? How's your mum?"

There is a pause at the other end of the line, followed by another slightly longer sigh.

"Becky?"

"Mum passed away."

There is silence in the flat. You reach out to turn on the lamp, as if better vision will somehow help you digest this news, but the light doesn't come on.

"When?" Your voice comes out almost as a croak.

"Just now, about ten minutes ago. I've only just come out of her room to let the hospital staff tend to her."

There is a gentle thud from the kitchen, the sound of something wet and only partially solid hitting the tiled floor. All other sound is deadened to you, other than the sound of Becky's breathing, and a faint, shivering hiss like a rattlesnake in the corridor.

"Are you still there?"

Your only response is a low whimpering, as the rushing sound of something unraveling comes sweeping and skittering down the corridor towards the bedroom, leafy fingernails dragging along the walls.

"You see?" Becky says, hearing you sobbing. "I knew you'd come around eventually…"

Conjuring the Man

Charlotte Byrne

Angie told me that what goes around comes around. It was when we were sitting in the common room among the empty cans of coke and magazines that I realised that there was no other way to make things right—I had to make Ty hurt.

Every time I closed my eyes I saw that cow's ankles around Ty's neck. Ingrained in my mind in the highest definition you could imagine. Stacey Springer, the class slag. He tried to apologise at first, a pathetic shadow of a man. Not even a man, a boy. A smelly boy with microscopic parts that never even did anything for me if we're getting down to it. I only loved him. He dropped me like a hot sausage, and now that she was carrying his seed they were looking for a ring. Their lives were over, but I felt like the one who was really suffering.

The free period between Art and Spanish seemed the perfect time to work out the plan, and Pearl didn't disappoint me when she flounced in.

"What have you brought?" I nodded at the carrier bag she had screwed up between her chipped nails. She patted it and I heard her bracelets jangle.

"Tomi, this will be the solution to all your problems."

"Will it help her pass Maths?" Angie snorted through her nose ring, and snatched the bag from her. She caught my eye and we both fought to hold back the giggles.

"Less it, you two. I'm trying to help you, Ayotomi." I sobered up. Not even my parents used my full name, even when they were cross.

Angie emptied the bag with a thump that made the Reems on the far side of the room look up from their phones and nail varnishes. I shot Angie daggers—nobody could know about this.

"Sorry," she huffed. She pawed the book that had fallen out and examined it. "£1.99? She wants revenge, not its poor relative."

"Doesn't matter." Pearl pushed her glasses up her nose. "A spell's a spell."

I bristled, still not comfortable with her magical answer for everything.

I needed action, not whimsy. She had to stop this. "I thought Wicca went out with Nu metal?"

Pearl smiled in that condescending way she has when she knows things that will make you look stupid.

"This isn't a *Wiccan* spell," she breathed over the doodled table. It didn't sound good. I opened my mouth to ask her what the deal was, but Mrs. Patel stormed in then, her floaty tops all aflutter.

"Sorry, girls, you'll have to reconvene in the IT suite. I've booked this room for the Year Sevens' tea party."

It's Friday night, and the rest of the Year Twelves are probably dolling themselves up to try and get into the club where the uni boys prowl. Angie and I are sitting in Pearl's bedroom with mugs of tea in our hands and all her weird music playing from her laptop. We've had psychedelic rock through metal, and now some girl with a piano is singing about abuse. You know, the deep stuff. Earlier, Angie called it 'music to kill yourself by' and I nearly choked on my Domino's. Pearl maintains it's essential to have angst-fuelled music for the spell to work. Something about reflecting the mood of the invoker. Though I don't feel angsty. I feel confused. I want to stop all this before we get in too deep.

I hear footsteps outside the room and Angie and I look up from our game of Scrabble as she creeps in.

"It's all good, everyone's out." She sits next to us and pushes the game board aside. "Time to conjure the Man."

I hesitate. "What man?"

Pearl rolls her eyes. "*The* Man. He's the one who's going to make things all right."

Angie snorts. "Bollocks. I know some blokes that would have sorted him out for you, Tomi."

"Ever the optimist, Ange," Pearl winces.

I want to intervene, but a scratching at the window makes me gasp. I glance at it and see the branches from the tree outside, shaking like scared kids in the rain. It's been hammering down for hours. Whether it's the horror movie weather, or some part of me not really wanting to see him get hurt, I swallow hard.

"Listen, Pearl. I'm not so sure I want to do this."

"You're not scared, are you?" Pearl looks at me over her glasses like a teacher. I shrink.

"I know it's your thing and everything, but…I don't know. Perhaps Ty will be happy with Stacey. I can't take that away from him."

It's the worst thing I could have said, but it needed to be out. My girls are reeling.

"Okay, even if it is bollocks, you have to do it now," Angie is up in my face. It's her own special way of looking out for me. "You need to get Ty out of your system."

Pearl takes my hand and rubs it. Her fingers are soft. "I promise you, it's perfectly safe. My room has been smudged and I've got sage on the windowsill."

I don't know what that means. I know that they're trying to make me feel better. I'm sweating, but it's only partly because of the fleece onesie I'm rocking. I wish I wasn't here, and that I was on the Reems' quest to snare uni boys, or curled up at home eating my own weight in Häagen-Dazs with the dog. Anywhere where I didn't have to think about my feelings.

"If it will make you feel better, I can leave the lights on when we conjure." Pearl is at the dimmer switch, ready to turn it up, but I shake my head.

"It's Stacey fucking Springer, Tomi," Angie tells me with a hand on my thigh. "Slaggy Springer. There's no way she loves Tyrone. And you don't want him back after what he's done. You're a mess. You have to do this." She holds the book in her lap and meets Pearl's worried eyes. "Even just to make you feel better."

"She's right. Think of it as closure."

I look at them, my girls. My BFFs if I'm going down that whole acronym route. They want to do what's right for me.

"Okay, whatever," I sigh, crossing my legs. "It can't hurt. It probably won't even work."

Pearl smirks and sits down on the rug again, nearly catching the Scrabble board. Angie gives me a pat on the knee and settles, seemingly prepping herself for this moment. All of us are silent. Ready, but not wanting to be the first to speak.

Pearl takes up the book, still with its price sticker on the cover, and opens it between her knees. I pull at the fleece material on my knee and start twisting it into a cone, letting it drop, then twisting again. It makes me feel a bit better.

The wind is getting up again as Pearl sets her candles out, perfectly arranged in a circle. It's starting to look like a real witches' hideout in here, even a cheap one. The music has gone quiet and the lights flicker before Angie leaps up and turns them off. Pearl is using a disposable lighter to light the candles, and they ignite quickly. Already the wax is starting to run and despite the heat and the tea and my onesie, I shiver. The dark envelops us, and the glow of the candles is warm but leaves me cold.

"Join hands."

Angie joins us again, and Pearl reaches out for her hand. I rub my palms on my knees before she grabs mine. Pearl's grip is firmer than I thought her capable of. She inhales deeply and gives me a ghost of a smile before looking down at the book on her knees and speaking.

"*Oh come, oh come—*"

"Emmanuel!" Angie chimes in and cracks up, slapping the carpet.

"Fuck *off*, Angie! You're not allowed to break the circle."

Angie bites on her lower lip, her face impish in the candlelight.

"S'broken now," she observes.

I giggle, for the first time in ages. Even Pearl can't resist a grin before clipping her with her bangled hand. "Do it properly, or go home. You can't mess around with this stuff."

Angie looks at me and I try to make my eyes plead without looking like a baby animal. She caves and grabs our hands again. Pearl bows her head and I'm sure she would close her eyes like a mad schoolteacher mid-speech if she didn't have to look at the book. Her mouth opens, and it begins:

"*Oh come, oh come, three times come.*
You who have power, let deeds be done.
We invoke you, sir. Hear our plea:
Bring that which is owed come to be."

I duck as lightning strikes and thunder shakes the house. It'd be hilarious in a horror movie, especially with the branches before. And the lights. It's all too obvious. The others don't seem to notice my shock.

"Have you got the photo?" Pearl looks at me expectantly. I don't want the circle to break again so I shimmy to the left and use my foot to kick it towards the centre.

It's not a flattering picture of either of us. It was taken in front of the rollercoaster at ThrillWorld. I've got ice cream around my face and a double chin due to the angle, and Ty is making a vulgar sign. It was a good day, though. We had our first proper kiss on the ghost train.

They know I'm lingering, so Pearl blows it into the fire and ThrillWorld is gone, swallowed by the burning wicks. The flame turns black. It looks black. There's a face in the blackness. Teeth? It could have been a reflection from the photo. Everything blows out and there is silence. My mind is blown, but surprisingly light. Perhaps this is a cleansing ritual. Perhaps it's what it's all about—Pearl never did explain exactly what the spell is.

Her voice breaks the still. "You saw him, didn't you?"

I swallow. *Play it cool*, I think.

"Saw what?" I drop their hands and jump up to turn the light on. "Right, whose Netflix are we gonna use?"

The bell rings, and the younger years all run down the corridor to their respective form rooms like the devil's after them. For us sixth-formers it's an irritating inconvenience, seeing as we don't go to registration. Worse for those that are hanging out of their arses. It's an inconvenience for me especially. Half an hour until our meeting with the head of sixth, and I'm alone collecting my things from my locker. It's creepy, like when you're in school for parents' evening and you need to go to the toilet and there's nobody around. It's wrong.

There's a tapping noise on the locker next to me. I push my locker door to, expecting to see one of the Reems ready to pick on me. Normally it's something along the lines of how I'm too pretty to still be hanging around with freaks like Angie and Pearl. Normally I reply by telling her to go fuck herself, or himself if it's one of their boyslaves. This time, there's nobody there.

I look up the corridor, an endless void. There's a shadow at the very end, next to the Drama board. It looks familiar, like it might be a person. I squint to try and work out who's there, but somebody sweeps past it and it's gone. It was never there.

Shit. It's Ty, coming towards me. His tie is untied and swinging around his neck like a limp sloth as he walks. His eyes are on the floor, and he's cracking his knuckles systematically. He always does when he gets nervous. They popped like an orchestra of Pringles cans when he broke up with me.

I focus on my bag and my textbooks and bury my head in the locker, hoping like an idiot that he hasn't spotted me. I hear the footsteps stop the other side of the door and more cracking. Neither of us speaks. An especially loud crack prompts me to give up.

"What do you want?" I direct it to my art folder in the corner.

"I have to talk to you," he mumbles.

I shove my Maths book into my bag and fiddle with the zip. "Can't it wait? I've got a class."

Lies, but I can't be talking to him now. I've been on a cloud all over the weekend and really knuckled down with my coursework. I even had time to shop with the girls. He can't drag me down now, but he insists on having his way.

"Me and Stace…Tomi, you know I never liked the girl. Don't like blondes."

I can't resist it. It's going to sound so cool. "Should've thought of that before you decided to shag her. Enjoy the rest of your life. Just get out of mine." End of conversation, as far as I'm aware.

"Listen, it's not my baby," Ty pleads. I'm sure he's trying to make me feel better, but it's not working. I don't know what to believe any more, whether to take his word as gospel like before, or whether to disbelieve everything that issues from his cheating lips.

"What do you mean it's not your baby?" I'm trying to play it safe. Not drop myself in it. But I'm curious to know if he means what he's saying.

"It's…not mine," he shrugs.

I put my textbooks down and turn to look at him. "How do you know?"

"She's…there was another guy around the same time." He looks embarrassed, but all I want to do is laugh. "It didn't mean anything."

No. No chance. Still, I listen as he continues.

"Tomato…" I fight it, but I have to smile on the inside. It's the first time I've heard him say my pet name in months. "I still love you, bae."

The smile's gone. I hate that word. Worse than 'YOLO' or 'fleek'. He's expecting an answer. What can I say? I can't say much. I don't want to say the wrong thing, or take him back, or do any of the stupid things girls are supposed to do under pressure. I need control, and I need to think.

"I'm gonna get some cigs from the offie," I lie. I try to act aloof as I shut my locker and storm past him. I don't look back, but I can hear the squeak of his non-uniform trainers as he follows.

Mrs. Patel says something as I walk past her in reception, but I don't hear what it is. I need to get away from him, just until I know how I feel. He says nothing, but I can still hear him behind me.

I look out at the school field across the road. The shadow's back, standing by one of the goals. I know he's watching me. This is what we did. He's here for Ty.

I step out by the traffic lights. I don't see the car.

Punishment

Andrew L. Huerta

Jonathan Early woke up in the back of an abandoned wooden cart. The cart served as his temporary prison, with brittle hay lining the floor, wooden slats constructing the three walls around him, an open back revealing only darkness outside, and no roof above. He rolled forward, on his side, and blinked his eyes back into focus. His hands and feet were bound by a thin rope that held his wrists and crossed ankles together. His hot breath dampened the white handkerchief that gagged his mouth, and he lifted his head up as far as he could.

Jonathan stared at a small space that ran between the boards at the side of the cart. He could feel the wind on his face, but he could not lift his head high enough to look out. With all of his strength, he pushed his body up but quickly lost his balance and fell backward. He bumped his head against the floor of the cart and rolled over on to his side. After several different attempts, Jonathan was able to push his upper body closer to the side of the cart. When he could finally sit up straight, he relaxed his arms and legs and tried to catch his breath. His gag had become drenched with sweat, spit, and blood, and Jonathan breathed heavily through his nose, trying not to vomit.

Jonathan turned his head and peered through the small space between two wooden slats. Darkness covered most of everything, but the sun had not set, and a faint light illuminated the tops of the trees. He looked up and saw an orange sky framed by dark green pine trees. He lowered his eyes and stared at the rope that bound his hands and feet together. All he could do now was sit there and wait. Wait and see for himself what Judge White always referred to as the Devil's Beast.

Jonathan knew that prisoners sentenced to death by Judge White would be taken out into the woods and left for the Devil's Beast. How anyone had come to know about the beast had been a mystery in town for generations. All Jonathan knew was that if a man committed a crime worthy of death, Judge White would always sacrifice him to the Devil's

Beast. The Judge always said how the town needed to appease the beast, so he would sentence the worst offenders to be left out in the woods to wait for their final punishment. The Judge said that if the beast were not fed as often as possible, it would surely come into town looking for victims.

Jonathan rested his head on the side of the cart and listened to the sounds of the night. The orange sky had faded to black, the sound of crickets grew louder, and the wind blew stronger through the top of the trees.

Jonathan heard a small noise behind him and jerked his head to one side. He lowered one eye to look through the wooden slats but only saw darkness. He heard something in the distance, and it sounded like the branches of a tree being snapped off. Jonathan pressed his back up against the side of the cart, waiting for the noise again, but there was only silence. He straightened himself up and tried desperately to place his feet flat on the floor to see if he could walk, but fell to his side, bumping his shoulder once again.

The pain in his shoulder was sharp, and he rested his head down on the floor of the cart. Every few seconds, Jonathan could hear something out in the woods. He lay still, listening to every sound. He could recognize the faint sound of footsteps that were quick and short. Whatever was out in the woods would quickly scurry toward him and then all of a sudden stop and wait. Jonathan heard the footsteps directly behind him, and he lifted his head to see what was there. He stared into the darkness, and heard more footsteps to his side, and then behind him once again. Whatever this beast was, Jonathan now knew that it was circling him. His heart beat so strongly that he was sure the beast could hear it. Jonathan's breathing grew stronger, and he wished that he could bite right through the gag and scream as loud as he could. He moved his head from side to side, looking into the darkness for anything at all. But he could still see nothing. Jonathan took a deep breath and held it. He was surrounded by silence, but he could feel the beast staring at him from somewhere in the distance.

"Hmmm…." Jonathan heard. His head jerked to one side. "Pri…son… er," the beast mumbled.

Jonathan rocked back and forth as he listened to the words of the beast. He began to wonder if the beast was actually a man, and if this man was going to kill him. Maybe there was no beast at all. Maybe Judge White left prisoners out in the woods to simply scare them. And maybe the Judge sent a man from town to terrorize the prisoners who were left out in the woods. Maybe he called that man the Devil's Beast to simply keep the people in town scared. Maybe the Devil's Beast was simply a man from town who would kill the prisoners and bury their bodies somewhere in the forest. Jonathan anticipated seeing a man at the back of the cart with a shotgun in his hands. But he saw nothing. He tried to scream through his gag, to make this man reveal himself, but it only came out as a muffled cry.

From out of nowhere, Jonathan saw a dark figure fly over him. He could feel its long nails scratch into the side of his face. All Jonathan could see was a dark image fly from one side of the cart to the other. Once it was gone, he could feel the deep gash that had been left at his jaw. With another loud scream, Jonathan was able to spit out his gag. He realized that not only had the side of his face been cut, but the beast had also cut clean through the handkerchief that gagged his mouth. Jonathan felt the warm blood running down his neck. He tilted his head and pushed the bloody handkerchief off his face.

"Help me, God!" Jonathan cried. He tried to catch his breath but stopped and waited to see the beast again.

"Your god cannot help you now," the beast whispered.

Jonathan frantically turned his head, trying to catch a glimpse of who or what was torturing him. He knew now that he would surely die, and he prayed that the beast would just show itself, and it would be over. Jonathan held his breath but still heard nothing. He exhaled slowly and rested his head back down again. After another moment of silence, Jonathan cried out, "Who are you?"

"I am the Devil's Beast," he heard from nowhere. A strong wind began to blow, and a dark figure appeared before him.

The beast stood still and then revealed to Jonathan its long talon-like fingernails. Jonathan watched as the claws reached toward him and slashed at the rope. The beast pulled its hands away and stared down at him. Jonathan looked back up and saw the beast to be half man and half animal. Most of its body was covered with thick, dark fur, and it stood in the darkness just a short distance away. Jonathan noticed that the beast was also dressed in rags that hung from its body. But as the clouds moved farther away from the moon, all Jonathan could focus on were the eyes of the beast. They were perfectly round and bright yellow in the center, while the sides appeared to be bloodshot, colored with a dark unnatural red.

With a quick jump, the beast flew out of sight and left Jonathan with blood and scratches covering his wrists and ankles. Jonathan pulled his hands and feet free and quickly crawled into the darkness in one corner of the cart. He waited for the beast and stared blankly at the forest in front of him. Not knowing what else to do, Jonathan jumped to his feet and flew off the back of the cart. He ran wildly toward the dark trees, but he could sense that the beast was somewhere close. He stopped running and looked into the forest. The light of the moon dimly lit everything around him, but all he could see was the cart and tall pine trees in every direction. He turned himself completely around and saw the bright yellow eyes in front of him. He took a few steps back and then sprinted for the cart. As he ran faster, something flew out of nowhere and knocked him to his knees. Jonathan brushed his hands around in the dirt and tried to find the yellow eyes once again, but they were nowhere in sight. Turning his head from side to side, Jonathan began to crawl toward the cart. When he had moved no farther than a foot, the wind blew again and he was knocked over onto his side. Jonathan looked down at his hands, covered in dirt, and began to cry. With all of his courage, he decided to stop running.

"What do you want from me?" Jonathan shouted.

"I will kill you, Prisoner," a voice replied.

Jonathan looked up and saw the beast standing at the side of the cart. All he could make out was a dark figure with bright, menacing eyes staring back at him.

"Then do it," Jonathan replied, spitting into the dirt.

"But I want to play first," the two eyes whispered back.

"If you're going to kill me, just do it. I don't wanna play." Jonathan placed his hands over his face and cowered down into the dirt.

"You are no meal for me!" The beast took a few steps forward, but Jonathan continued to hold his face down toward the ground. "I will eat your flesh and drink your blood, but you are just a boy." Jonathan uncovered his face and slowly looked up into the eyes of the beast. "They have never sent me someone as small as you. What did you do, boy?"

The beast turned his hand out toward Jonathan, and his talons appeared white and glowing in the moonlight.

Jonathan stared into the eyes of the beast, and his shoulders tensed as the beast stepped forward. The beast had the pale-white-face of death, with bright yellow eyes and jagged, razor-sharp teeth. His face appeared to be that of a man, yet his body was slightly hunched over with long arms and strong, thick legs. His feet were long and thin, but his large hands appeared to be human, with curved talons ending in sharp tips. The beast tilted his head to one side and waited for Jonathan to answer.

"I…" Jonathan began, "I didn't do anything wrong."

"Then why are you here?" The beast held his hands out in front of him, as if he were unable to lower them to his sides. "And why don't you want to play?"

"I don't know why I'm here, and I don't feel like playing." Jonathan lowered his head.

"Then I will take you to my cave, and you will stay with me until you feel like playing."

"What will we play?" Jonathan asked sternly, as he looked up from the ground and gazed at the beast's face.

"You will run and hide, and I will come catch you."

"But I'm not good at games like that."

"It is a simple game, and I will teach you."

"I still don't wanna play." Jonathan watched as the beast turned his head away. The beast then smiled, revealing his jagged teeth, and gave a slight laugh.

"Then I will leave you here for now," he began again. "In the daylight, you will run down the road to town. You will never make it there by sundown. When the sun is down, I come out. I will find you before darkness, and we will play then."

"No," Jonathan replied, before the beast could turn away. "Kill me now, or I will kill myself before sunrise."

"What?" the beast shouted. His eyes widened, and Jonathan stared at the redness that surrounded the yellow at the center.

"I have nothing to live for. I have no family, and Nick Shepard lied and told everyone that I tried to kill his son." Jonathan stopped and remembered how Nick had almost beaten his own son to death. "I didn't do it! Samuel is my friend, and no matter what they say, I didn't do it."

"Do what?" The beast tilted his head.

"Hurt Samuel!" Jonathan stared at nothing and shook his head. "Nick did it. Nick did it because he saw us together."

"Nick Shepherd?" The beast appeared to relax and took one step away from Jonathan. "I have heard his name before."

"Nick sent me here."

"Here to die?" The beast lowered his hands, but still held them at a distance from his sides.

"Yes," Jonathan replied.

"You must have done something wrong. What did you do wrong?"

"I told you!" Jonathan watched the beast turn away. "I've done nothing wrong! They just want to keep us apart."

The beast looked over at the cart and then turned back toward Jonathan. "Everyone who is brought here has done something wrong. If you did not do it, then who did the wrong that you are being punished for?"

"Nick." Tears rolled down Jonathan's face.

After a few seconds of silence, the beast raised his hands, stared down at Jonathan, and asked, "Is this Nick a large man?"

"Nick is too strong for me." Jonathan lowered his head to the ground.

"Nick might be fun to play with, wouldn't he?"

"Yes," Jonathan whispered, as he stared at the beast's thick legs.

"Would I have fun with Nick?"

"Yes, you would." Jonathan looked up at the beast's hands.

"Would you take me to Nick?"

"Yes," Jonathan said, as he gazed into the eyes of the beast and smiled.

"Show me the man you hate so much that you would bring me to this place," the beast said, after Jonathan had led him to the Shepard's farm. Jonathan stood at the edge of a short path with the beast just a few feet behind him.

Jonathan looked up at the beast and walked closer to the house. "Follow me."

They walked to the back door of the house but found it locked. Jonathan looked back at the beast, who stepped in front of him, and pulled the door off of its hinges. They both stepped inside and found

Nick's son, Samuel, asleep in the back room.

"This is the one you fear so much?" The beast stood over Samuel and stared down at the boy's bruised and beaten body.

"No," Jonathan replied. He sat down on the side of the bed. "This is my friend, Samuel. Samuel is Nick's son, and Nick is the one who tried to kill him."

"What the…" Nick screamed, as he stood in the doorway and saw Jonathan and the beast standing over his son.

In the blink of an eye, the beast was on Nick and grasped him tightly around the throat. He raised him up in the air and smiled.

"This is the man?" the beast asked.

"Yes," Jonathan replied and looked back down at Samuel.

"He will be a fine meal." The beast examined Nick as he held him higher in the air. "And we will have a wonderful time playing together, won't we?" The beast lowered Nick's face and scratched his nose with a sharp talon. Nick fainted in his grasp.

"I will take him back to the forest." The beast turned and stared at Jonathan.

"And will you ever come back for me?" Jonathan looked up from Samuel but continued to stare at the back wall.

"No," the beast replied. "I will never come back to punish you." The beast stared at Nick, limp and lifeless in his hand. He walked out the door, and Jonathan could hear him dragging Nick's body across the field. Jonathan sat there and listened until there was silence once again.

"Jonathan," Samuel whispered, after several hours.

"I'm here," he replied. Samuel's eyes fluttered open and looked up at his friend.

"Where's my father?" Samuel sat up and began to look around frantically.

"Hell," Jonathan replied. He placed his hands on Samuel's shoulders and eased him back down on the bed. "The Devil came, and he took your father to Hell."

The Factory

Sarah K. Stephens

blame everything that happened later on craft service. If their tables hadn't been so deliciously laden with oozing pasteurization and overripe but tantalizing rogue strawberries, I would now be on the next set or the next table or whatever, none the wiser. But I had hovered over and hoovered the edible offerings, and I had bumped into, mouth full of my favorite cheese/cracker/summer sausage combo, the person who would shred the thin veil between myself and the world that this place had deigned I be allowed to shroud myself in, like a velour hoodie. Soft and unflattering, and just as easily cast off.

When I met Candace, her name should have sent a pang of alertness through my spine. 'Call me Candy,' she'd said, extending in greeting her soft palm across the bran muffin platter (untouched by all) after I mumbled an apology through the chalky residue always left in my mouth by processed meat. I ate it anyway.

Candy asked the question everyone asks on set. "Cast or crew?"

When I first started this job, my answer had needed some massaging, seeing as I didn't view myself as the traditional sort of player.

"Cast for the crew," was what I finally landed on. Honestly, despite my effort, most people didn't even go further than that, already bored once I went on to amend 'cast.' For those who did, like Candy, my explanation continued, "I handle the needs for the crew."

I tried to say it with some salacious tinge embedded inside the words, and Candy gave an appreciative eyebrow raise in reply. I didn't feel the need to clarify that most of the needs involved sandwich shop runs for the gaffer (in my experience, most of these guys never wanted to touch craft service—instead, I had to travel 30 minutes to get a grinder at some shop owned by a friend of a friend) or scheduling chiropractor appointments for the grips. I hadn't been touched intimately by an actual man in over a year.

"What about you?" Now, when I scan my memory backwards, I see this as where I made my mistake, where the arrows pointing my life in one direction veered off-course and skittered into the guardrail.

"Oh," here, I swear to God, Candy blushed scarlet red and put her hand to her chest, like she couldn't believe I was asking her about herself. "Well, I'm Devon and Diana's mom."

Candy waited expectantly now, her mouth puckered open as I tried to figure out who she was talking about. I noticed a thick strap poking out of her shirt's neck-hole, the beige fabric interrupted just above her collarbone with a rigid flap of material fastened like a tent door. It was a nursing bra.

"Oh, the babies in the Thanksgiving meal scene—right?"

Candy nodded her head, ending in a bashful tuck of her chin. I realized she was waiting for something else.

"They're such good girls," I offered, trying to recall from my mind how they'd been when they were on set last week. The shot had taken an entire two days because labor laws required so many breaks and trade-offs between the twins (something about light exposure) with the hired nurse checking on them in-between each take. My coffee run had taken over an hour—that's right, the key grip liked fancy coffee too—and they'd still been on the same scene number when I got back. I'd worked on twenty sets already, and this was the first to have any babies involved.

Candy swatted playfully at my shoulder and I could feel the smooth square edges of her nails tracing the fabric of my shirt. She had a great manicure. "Oh, aren't you sweet. They're just getting so big!"

Today's scene was one with nude doubles and a few close-ups of the principals' faces looking ecstatic.

"Are they doing a re-shoot or something today?" My mind worried back to the sides sent around this morning, announcing the shot list for the day. I'd only glanced at them.

Candy had been reaching out for a tuna sandwich on wheat, to go with her brownie and slathering of Nutella on the side. Her hand paused in mid-air, as if my question stretched out and nipped at her wrist.

Turning towards me, I could see the corners of her mouth tilt upwards into a smile, the thin lines around her mouth cracking open wider. Not for the first time, I wondered how old Candy was. Anywhere between an ill-kempt 27 and a well-maintained 48, I figured.

"I came in to meet with Martin"—Martin was the director—"to talk about something, and he asked me to stay on set and watch the scenes for today. Give him my opinion."

A little conditioned 'ping' went off in my brain, and I tried to look at Candy differently.

I didn't want to be the sandwich girl (yeah, yeah, yeah—cast for the crew, my ass—I knew what I was) for the rest of my career. I set down my plate and, with all the social finesse I could muster, tried to climb up.

"How could you have twins and still be so…" My mind failed me here for a moment, instead recalling only words like 'cheap' and 'wilted,' until it clicked back into rotation. "So culturally involved."

It was the best I could come up with.

I must have sounded a little desperate because Candy smiled, more sincerely this time, almost conciliatory with her upturned chin and crinkly eyes, and complimented me for my sweetness again before launching into her explanation of how she was in desperate need for a babysitter tomorrow night. Her husband and she wanted to attend a dinner party thrown by Martin, and their babysitter had canceled last minute.

"You seem like a very nice, responsible young woman." I recalled my earlier allusion to satisfying the crew. "I bet you love children!"

"Absolutely. I used to babysit all the time back home."

"Fantastic. Our house, 7 o'clock." As she got my phone number from me and texted over her address, I tried to ignore the voices of experience in my head, of my sister and my Aunt Judith and our neighbors growing up, chorusing that good mothers asked for credentials first before anyone went near their babies. Instead, I read over my own backstory for motivation.

I wanted my own sandwich girl.

Taking her plate with her, the contents covered in a paper napkin like old women do with church picnic leftovers, Candy offered her hand again before heading out. It was sweaty.

"I'd better go give Martin my notes." She looked me straight in the eye, her brown irises depthless. "He and I go way back, you know."

And then she winked.

Candy lived in a small pink stucco house that seemed to be the

building equivalent of a perm. Bedraggled rose bushes and a yard consisting of river rock with weeds tumbling out of the crevices framed the small dwelling. I'd driven by Martin's house once, while out on one of my Italian melt runs. Walking up this woman's cracked sidewalk path to the front door, which boasted a twig wreath with winterberries poking out at odd angles as if a bird had tried to grab them and run for it, I doubted whether Candy would have anything to wear to dinner at Martin's. Nothing in my own closet would have worked, and I didn't have maternal instincts suffocating my need to be 'with it.'

Someone opened the door before I had the chance to knock, giving me the distinct impression that the house was on the lookout for me. The man who ushered me in was small and dark featured, like an extra from a Scorsese film. He had shifty eyes that never once settled on my face—they just kept darting around to random points, like they were tracing a flying insect's attempt to escape this cool, dark house.

The door opened into a small hall with a coat hanger and dingy gray tiles that led into the kitchen/living room, the two distinct from each other by a half-wall covered in papers and discarded diaper boxes. The man introduced himself as Don Ruggiero, Candy's husband. Don's shirt was open one button too many at the top. He rubbed his nose with his right hand, pinching his septum between his thumb and index finger, before calling for his wife. His voice was higher in pitch than mine.

Candy trailed in from the right through the sparse living room. She was in a dress that was a size too small, highlighting her leftover baby roundness below her breasts with its clingy red fabric. It must have been something she owned before she got pregnant. I'd seen women do this before—cast, mostly, wishing to retrograde their decision and camouflage their lives into something less potent.

I caught Don giving his wife an appreciative glance, his line of sight stopping suddenly on the soft curves of her belly, and I felt immediately chastened.

Candy smiled at me in greeting and, pulling on her coat, gave my instructions.

"Numbers are on the fridge. The girls are resting in their cribs—first door on the left." She tilted her head down the hall spanning out from the kitchen, on the opposite side of the house from where she'd come from. She called over her shoulder as Don ushered her out the door, interrupting my questions.

"The older kids are in their room—they'll be fine on their own. And I'll be sure to tell Martin what a great job you do." Wink, her blue eye shadow creasing in the folds of her right eyelid, and she was gone.

The door closed with a soft click, its wooden body fitted perfectly into the frame of the house. It gave no resistance as it closed me inside.

Their car turned away to wherever they were going, its rumble fading into the ambient sound of the house. I stood for a moment, listening to the silence of this home that was supposedly full of children. My ears perked as the ice dropped in the freezer. The soft murmur of the ceiling fan in the living room filtered towards me from both sides.

I went over to the sink in the kitchen to wash my hands first, a habit formed years ago. The sink was steel, with two basins. Yellow prescription bottles and vials addressed to 'Candace Ruggiero' were littered against the splashboard. I didn't recognize any of the labels.

I headed into the babies' room first, assuming they were my main charges for the night. I opened the door slowly, remembering that young children are afraid of strangers, and cursed myself for trying to take shortcuts.

The room was a breath of freshness; little clouds of fragrance wafted through the room. Baby powder. Sugar. Detergent. Everything inside was white: walls, curtains, cribs. Even the little girls' nightgowns were pristine. The cribs were pushed into each other at a 90-degree angle in the back corner of the room.

Devon and Diana (I didn't even know which was which) were soundly sleeping in their beds. I could hear the small intake of their breaths, both of their mouths pursed into unnaturally red buds. It reminded me of summers, sucking on popsicles, or cough medicine's sticky residue. I closed the door behind me, thankful that they appeared content.

The hall was dark, lit only from the small patch of yellow seeping out from underneath the final door.

The older kids, I repeated to myself. *They'll be fine on their own.*

I walked down towards the door, unsure of what I planned to do once I reached the end. My steps ricocheted against the walls, the worn carpet underneath my feet failing to soften the fact that I didn't belong there.

Suddenly, my eyes blinked and it was entirely dark. The light beneath the door had been extinguished, although I hadn't heard any of the telltale sounds of children trying to hide their misdeeds. Giggles. Tiny feet trampling across the floor. Covers rushing up to chins.

I knocked on the door. "Hello?"

My voice squeaked unattractively, making me sound younger than I was. Perhaps that was a good thing. Looking back, I don't know if anything I did or didn't do in that house could have made a difference.

Only empty silence answered me back.

I reached out and turned the doorknob, swinging the door open with the same ease the front door had as it shut. Inside, I was met with the smell of unwashed skin and unbrushed teeth. A children's sleepover gone on for too many days.

There were three sets of bunk beds, six beds each. Two were pushed against each wall, the third shoved against and blocking the one window in the room. I thought automatically that the children sleeping there would be too cold come winter, but remembered that I wasn't home. Winter never arrived in this place.

I flipped on the light. The brightness must have been a shock to their eyes, even though they'd just extinguished the light a few moments ago, because they squinted and pinched their faces. The ones by the window both pulled their blankets up in what I assumed was unplanned symmetry.

None of them spoke. Three sets of faces looked back at me, two to each bunk bed. Three pairs of twins. Two were boys, on the left and right. The girls slept by the window. They looked the oldest, but I was only guessing at their age. They didn't smile, so I couldn't see their teeth, and their bodies were covered by blankets. It was just a gut feeling.

At least until I recognized them.

When I was in high school, there was a sitcom about a foster family. It'd been really popular—all the boys in school were obsessed with the one daughter who didn't seem to wear a bra—and it had been on for a few seasons before vanishing by the time I graduated. One of the trademarks of the show was this little girl who would repeat the same phrase each episode at random spots to canned laughter. My parents had commented that she was the real star.

The girls looked back at me, mirroring each other in the top and bottom bunks. The one on top seemed to register that I'd recognized her. Her jaw slackened a bit, as if she were chewing on her tongue.

Then, in a scratchy voice, she said, "What*ever*." Her two hands pulled up into the double V's she'd made on camera, years ago. My eye caught a movement from the bottom, and I saw her twin mimic the same sign.

The boys stayed in their beds, unmoving.

After pausing for a moment, I turned around and left the room, closing the door quietly behind me. Before I could move further down the hallway, I heard a dull thump against the door and the light flickered for a moment before the hallway went dark again. By the time Candy and Don returned home, I'd spent four hours sitting in their silent house biting my nails and waiting for something to happen.

I never checked what the thump had been.

The next day I avoided Candy's voicemails. When I arrived at work, the entire crew were murmuring about the next project, complaining about the amount of kids that were going to be involved. It seemed Martin had already signed a few families, but they were looking for pregnant women to help flesh out the infant roles. Production started in 6 months.

I went to see the movie when it came out. By this time, I was back home working at my sister's preschool. I didn't recognize any of the kids, but I made sure to check the credits at the end. Baby Jane was played by Elena and Erica Ruggiero.

Atabey

Oliver Ledesma

In truth, I cannot recall with absolute certainty the events that had transpired all those months ago. When I arrived back at the village after fleeing through the night from Loma Soñador, the villagers only looked at me with a pitiful and understanding gaze. I'm sure they were more aware of what I had encountered on that night up in the mountains than I was. I was an outsider with no understanding of the world I was stepping into. But they lived here, this primal place where unexplainable things still thrived, away from the prying eyes of humanity.

That particular summer, after vacationing in the Dominican Republic, I ended with a visit to my grandmothers in Baní, a coastal city southwest of the capital Santo Domingo. I spent many of my childhood summers with her. My abuelita used to tell me stories to pass the time, stories of monsters like terrible Brujas that drink the blood of children, gorgeous Ciguapas that lure and eat men lost in the jungle, and cruel Biembiens living in the mountains of Bahoruco. Eccentricity is not a trait that ran deep in my family but it did in my abuelita.

It was during this summer that she recounted to me a different story that I had heard only a few times before in my youth. It was rumored by the people in the higher hills of the Dominican Republic that the Moon was different here. It was not merely an orbiting planetary body but an entity, the remnants of an old goddess of the Taino natives, seeking her vengeance on the people who have forgotten her. One night, in one of the many hilltop villages that dot the island, a young boy was sent to collect firewood for his family, but he ventured too far away from his village. That's when the Moon took her first sacrifice, swallowing the boy whole along with the firewood he carried. Abuelita swears that on clear summer nights she can still see the silhouette of a little boy carrying firewood on the face of the Moon. I always thought stories like these, while interesting, mainly served to keep children from straying too far from villages and that the markings on the Moon are nothing but craters and rocks that have played tricks on the minds of people around the world for millennia.

The story had reminded me, however, of my initial desire to see more natural parts of the Island, locations untainted by the expanse of civilization. I fancied myself a bit of a nature man and have hiked and camped in the U.S. before but never in my native land. Abuelita, of course, did not like the idea and though she was apprehensive at first, eventually relented and was on the phone the next minute to ask an old friend, Juan Duarte Herrera, if he would be available to act as a guide for my camping adventure. Though I had apparently spent many summers as a boy playing vitilla with Herrera, I hardly remembered him at all. She handed me the phone and after a short conversation, he agreed to take me up Loma Soñador, a relatively small but remote mountain he was familiar with some ways north of Baní for the price of 7000 pesos.

We set the day of the trip two days later on the 21st of July on the night of a Full Moon with the intention to hike and camp by moonlight. Those two days we did not lose focus and spent them preparing basic supplies like water, compasses, and headlamps. My confidence in my companion grew when he professed to know alternative routes and passes on the north side of the mountain that could cut our travel time in half and told of a village close to the starting trail where we could attain a pair of mules. He determined that the paths were of course much too overgrown and wild to drive up and that to even reach them we would need the assistance of mules. The path, however daunting it sounded, only strengthened my enthusiasm for I knew we were on the right track to see those beautiful natural vistas I had only dreamed about.

On the morning of the trip, Herrera arrived at my grandmother's in a gray dilapidated pick-up truck. He stepped out of the truck and handed me a machete to fasten to my belt explaining I would need it later. As we had quite the ride ahead of us, we wasted no time, only saying a quick farewell to my abuelita before the truck began to sputter away. It wasn't a long drive out of Baní as we were already situated on the outskirts of the city, however once we took the main road north past Villa Guera and toward Majaguita, the road abruptly turned to dirt and was engulfed by the jungle.

After 3 hours of twists and turns through endless green, there was no more road to follow as the jungle parted to a clearing of a few dozen crudely built homes with tin roofs. The villagers, or "campesinos" as Herrera called them, welcomed us with smiling faces and it was apparent that this village did not receive many visitors and there was little in the way of both excitement and opportunity here for them.

Despite my many summers and childhood with my abuelita, my Spanish fluency left much to be desired leaving the task of communicating with the campesinos to my handy guide and, after a few short conversations, we were directed to an elderly man with only a few good teeth who was all too glad to loan his mules off for a few pesos. However, when informed that we were to climb Loma Soñador, the smile on his face died and was replaced with a furrowed brow and worrisome stare. The elderly man and Herrera looked at each other for a second before exchanging a few words in Spanish I did not wholly understand except for a singular phrase tongued by the old man through his few good teeth. *"Si te ven, no te dejan ir."* A wide patronizing grin grew on Herrera's face before the man had finished speaking. He placed his hand on the poor man's shoulder and smiled. The near toothless old man locked his eyes onto mine and in his countenance was not a hint of the worrisome look he had previously worn but instead the look of a man filled with overwhelming pity.

As we rode out towards the northern side of the mountain, I inquired of my guide the meaning of the conversation that had just taken place as I was only able to glean from the elderly man's face that he was worried about something. While the mules continued down the sloping path deeper into the great silent green expanse of vegetation, Herrera turned to look me in the eyes and smiled another broad smile.

"The villagers are very superstitious. He was worried we might run into Ciguapas and that if they see us, they won't let us leave."

The mules, to their credit, were remarkably able animals that needed very little guidance to navigate the slopes and passages around to the north side of the mountain and I could scarcely imagine what the trail would have been like without their assistance. On muddy slopes, where I was sure we would have had trouble or at the very least an inconvenience, the mules steadily kept their footing and trudged on as if they had walked these trails all their life. When we arrived at a small clearing with what looked like a rudimentary hitching post, it was an indication that we were at the start of Herrera's shortcut. The mules could continue no further as these alternative trails were rife with overhanging branches, short palms, and other native flora that would have impeded us were it not for the machetes Herrera had us bring along. It was readily apparent that this path had not seen regular use and from this point on it was essentially no man's land. We decided it was safe to leave the mules tied to the hitching post and would return for them in the morning.

As we cut our way through the thick green labyrinth of untouched vegetation, Herrera informed me of the remoteness of the area. Though the paths leading to the hitching post were regularly used by the nearby villagers, the path we had now been ascending to the upper parts of Loma Soñador were not known to them and were a well-kept Herrera family secret. I had greatly underestimated how much willpower would be needed on this hike into uncharted territory and though I had been whacked in the face by a number of branches and palms already, I was nevertheless determined to see what sights we would encounter.

After the climb up a relatively steep hill about midway up the mountain, we came to a vast and great plateau on the northeastern face of Loma Soñador that was surely not visible from any other point in the valley. At this spot, we were treated to an astonishing and captivating view, the vast Dominican countryside. The Sun's rays extended as far out as the eye could see to other mountains and valleys in the distance covered by trees without a single trace of humanity. Far below us, the small clearing where the mules were hitched was only just barely visible. The realization that this path was undisturbed by men for decades had begun to dawn on me but had not fully set until we had traveled through another patch of trees to another small clearing and were greeted with a sight I could not have expected. There, high in the mountains of the Dominican Republic, with the sunlight filtering through open palm leaves, were a number of large granite slabs arranged neatly in a circular pattern surrounding a large singular boulder. We had stumbled upon an ancient Taino ruin. While I was well aware of the island's previous inhabitants before the Spanish landed and all but eradicated them, I had never heard of nor laid my eyes on such a well-preserved example of Taino culture surviving until the modern age. The stones were large and smooth, each marked with a different petroglyph depicting various

animals and symbols. However, the boulder in the center of the ruins had the same marking carved into each and every side of its faces, a depiction of a crouching woman with what looked like an intricate headdress. Upon closer inspection, the stones appeared free of both moss and any weathering they should have endured through their surely longstanding lifetime which made them seem less like well-preserved ruins and more like a well kept ritual site. Though it was Herrera's assumption that no one else knew of this area, the evidence overwhelmingly supported the contrary, a theory that grew prominence in our minds when we found footprints around the site. As interesting as the ruins were, we had no interest in meeting wayward villagers up in the mountains, so we left the site, heading in the opposite direction of the footprints, which were facing back towards the plateau.

At this point, neither my companion nor I had any notion of the world we were walking into or of the perils lurking deeper into the jungle. Feeling optimistic after the discovery of the ruins and relishing in the thought of what other wonders we could stumble upon, we failed to notice the sun sinking lower and lower into the sky and the Moon beginning its ascent. With the light fading, the verdant landscape had begun to grow dark and unwelcoming. The feeling of wonder had mutated into a creeping sense that we should have at this point, turned back and made camp, but instead we pressed on.

As we continued to delve deeper and deeper into uncharted territory, we heard the sound of crashing water, which Herrera stated must be a waterfall and would make the best possible spot for camp. When we edged closer to the site, however, more footsteps appeared pressed into the dirt, a singular trail heading away from the waterfall. Thinking the villagers must have been aware of the waterfall and made regular use of it, we pressed on confident that whoever it was, according to the footprints, had already left the area. Through the bushes I caught my first glimpse of those majestic falls, tall and resplendent and surrounded by trees on all sides all the way to the bottom that kept the location well hidden. It was yet another treasure, hidden away up high in the hills.

As I watched the water spill over the edge of the steep rocks and into the large natural basin at the bottom, I became enthralled by the sheer beauty of the place and began making my way through the foliage when Herrera pulled me to the side behind the bushes. His eyes widened as he placed one finger on his lips to signal silence and pointed to a dark shape in the water I had missed in my excitement over the falls. There, bathing in the middle of that hidden paradise, stood the most alluring creature, a woman, with dark brown skin submerged from the waist down in the water. Bathed in moonlight, her hair was black and endless as it flowed down over her breasts and over the curves of her back, into the water where it danced with every ripple. I turned to Herrera, intending to ask if he thought she was from the nearby village but had at once forgotten my question when I saw the look upon his face. He continued to point towards the woman and did not share my awe at this creature's beauty but instead wore a look of ghastly abhorrence that had drained all color from his face, which led me to believe the sight he had seen was not the same as the one I had. But when I turned my head back fully expecting to once again bask in the radiance of the maiden of the waterfall, I instantly took notice of what had shook my partner to the bone and left him in such a catatonic state. The woman's legs were inverted, her knees bent in an inhuman fashion and her feet faced backwards as she stepped out of the pool. It was all I could do to stifle a scream. It was no woman, but a ciguapa, a man-eating temptress of legend, and we had unwittingly tracked it here. I looked back to my partner and it seemed we were in accord. Deciding that we had had enough adventure for a lifetime, we fled. We ran through the jungle blindly and wildly as the words of the toothless old man echoed in my head, "If they see you, they won't let you leave."

We had to reorient ourselves and quickly find our way back to the mules. Staying out in the Dominican wilds was no longer an option lest we wanted to discover what other myths and legends were true. The plan was to head north, to find the great plateau again that overlooked the hitching post, hop on the mules and put as much distance between Loma Soñador and us as possible. However, north proved problematic to find for though the compass pointed us in the right direction, it also pointed directly at the Moon, which could not have been as the Moon travels through the southern sky. Yet the Moon was clearly in the same direction as the compasses pointer in the north at the time and while we could not reconcile that fact, we could at least deduce that the peak of Loma Soñador had always been to our right as we traveled into the jungle so we followed the compasses direction of north, putting the peak of that now looming dreadful mountain to our left as we traveled.

The moonlight that served to illuminate our path was now harsh and oppressive, revealing us when we wished to stay hidden. We had no choice but to continue to run towards the sinister spotlight whose new position in the sky had begun to instill a sense of irrational fear of the celestial body. A fear as potent as to play tricks on an already fearful mind for I could swear, appearing upon its large gray face, was now the silhouette of a boy carrying a bundle of sticks. Its haunting presence continued to loom over us as we ducked and dodged through the trees and branches we had earlier passed. The landscape, though dark, had begun to look familiar and I was certain we were heading in the right direction but as we got closer to the great plateau, something stopped me, a high-pitched chirping that made my blood run cold. It was my turn to place my hand on my companion's shoulder to stop his advance. We crouched down among the foliage once again and cautiously inched our way forward only to witness the terrifying source of the sound.

Illuminated by torches now placed at the forgotten Taino ruin were five of those beautifully horrible creatures, their exquisitely long hair nearly touching the ground as they pranced on those awful legs of theirs. Around the center boulder, one of their own yelled loudly in a language forgotten to time, chanting "ATABEY ATABEY" in a shrill chirping voice that filled the air while the rest danced in worship of the petroglyph of the crouching woman. We were, for the moment, completely hidden from sight of the creatures but the longer we stayed idle in those bushes, the more at risk we were of discovery. Therefore, we began to creep our way around the ruins, making absolutely certain to stay under the brush. However, it seemed the very jungle itself was against our escape, for we made it not halfway around the edge of the ruins before the leaves and twigs on the ground began snapping with a loud crack, betraying our location. When we peeked our heads over the brush to see if we had been discovered, we were met with five sets of eyes glaring back at ours. I watched in horror as the faces of those once heavenly creatures distorted into faces of utter madness resembling hellish ghouls. A terrible scream erupted from their mouths causing us to abandon all sense of subtlety and make a mad dash towards the plateau.

We dared not look back into the face of terror and continued our escape towards the great plateau but we could hear their shrill chirping behind us every step. When we arrived at the large clearing of the plateau, the fiends ceased their pursuit at the tree line and seemed afraid to step past it. As confusing as their abrupt stop was, I was infinitely more dumbfounded by the absence of what was once so prominent in the sky in front of us. That ominous sphere that shone so brightly only a few moments ago had disappeared, vanished from its abnormal position in the north. As portentous as its absence was, we could not afford to relent in our haste, nor did we as we continued our sprint across the great plateau.

It was then that my partner tripped over himself and, though I was a few steps ahead of him, my first instinct was to double back and assist my clumsy companion. But when I turned around, I realized it was a decision I would come to instantly regret. For what I witnessed in that moment, as Herrera raised his machete in a futile defense, would fill me with a restlessness and doubt that would haunt me for the rest of my years. I slid down the side of that plateau, filled with adrenaline and a newfound fervor, brought upon by that otherworldly sight, that when I finally reached the hitching post I was able to cut the tightly wound knot securing the mules with one fell swoop of the machete and rode through the night back to the village.

To this day, I cannot say exactly what it was that I saw during Herrera's final moments, as to put it in words would be to admit my insanity and have me committed. Regardless, I can no longer enjoy the night sky, which, while at one point it brought me great pleasure, now only fills me with a terrible dread and anxiety. This is only compounded by alarming recent reports from observers around the world of what seem to be new craters formed on the face of the Moon. While scientists and astronomers are baffled by the appearance of the new formation, I can only be absolutely horrified. For now, on the face of that ghastly floating orb in the sky, is the silhouette of a man with an iron machete raised in his hand.

Hunters

Jack Lothian

t dragged itself across the lawn, dirty, trembling, terrified. The night was cold, and it needed somewhere to hide. It could hear the laughter and shrieks of children from streets outside. The windows of the house were lit with orange lanterns. The sky was clear overhead, a blanket of stars above. It curled up in the shadow of the hedgerow, bleeding and shaking. It knew the end of was near.

The man was driving a station wagon, cruising along the suburban streets. He slowed down to let a ghost, a mummy and some superhero he didn't recognize cross the road in front of him. His fingers drummed impatiently on the wheel, and he had to fight the urge to hammer the horn, to hurry them up, especially when the superhero dropped his plastic pumpkin-head on the ground and its candy brains spilled out. The ghost and the mummy crouched down to help the hero retrieve his treasure.

He had been tracking it for months now. It traveled at night, slept in abandoned buildings or train yards during the day. He would lose the trail for weeks on end, but he kept going, methodical, thorough, just as his father had taught him. Three hours ago, he'd finally caught up with it.

It was hiding in the empty garages near the strip mall. He picked up the scent. It had taken years, but it had become second nature, his strange metallic odor that would hang heavy in the air for hours. You could even taste it, that's what his father had told him. Locked him in the basement with the body of one of them, hours after hours, until the stink was everywhere, in his nose, his lungs.

It was curled up, sleeping behind rusted machinery, waiting for the sun to sink down before it moved on again. The man had been foolish—he'd let his adrenaline control him, moving him in too fast, his boot crunching on broken glass, alerting it. There was barely time to react as it sprung awake and scrambled for the exit. He'd swung out, connecting, and it had pitched sideways, crashing into the worktop, but

its momentum allowed it to continue, barreling towards the door, out into the fading light, and by the time he'd regained balance and made it outside, it was gone.

He had hurt it though. But hurting it wasn't enough.

It would die tonight.

Tom had sneaked out of the house. His mother had told him he was grounded for the week, on account of Tom stealing twenty dollars from her bag, twenty dollars he'd put towards buying a video game where one could hunt down monsters across lush forest-land and ruined cities; something of an irony considering that the game's promise of unrivaled open exploration had led him to be confined to his bedroom. The window had a latch that was easy enough to open and there was only a short drop to the garden below. His friends were all out tonight, and he didn't want to be left out, even if he'd have to go without a costume.

He should have taken a sheet from the bed. He could have put it over his head at least, said he was some kind of ghost, no matter how lame that would be. On some level, he understood there wouldn't be many more nights like this. What seemed fun at eleven years old would be scorned and mocked by the time they were twelve. Even so, he could already feel something in the air; a sense of excitement, a sense that normal rules didn't apply on this one night of the year.

Tom was heading for the gate out of the back yard when he spotted it. At first he thought it was someone in a costume, maybe even one of his friends, waiting to play a trick on him. Tom decided that whatever happened, he wouldn't react, wouldn't be scared, in case someone was capturing all this on a camera phone and his shocked response ended up spreading far and wide across the net. Far better to act cool, shrug, like it was an everyday occurrence that some ghost or beast suddenly leaped up at you. That would show them.

With each step closer, Tom's certainty that this was some trick wavered a little. It looked like a man, but as if he'd been stretched and extended, so his arms and legs were almost spider like. Bald. Pale translucent skin. It briefly reminded him of some toy he'd had in kindergarten, half-forgotten now, some cheap plastic thing (*Stretcho Man? Expando Dude?*) but that had not had these sullen black eyes or a shivering wound for a mouth.

The creature was wheezing, weak. The puncture wound in its chest made every gasped breath a struggle. The frantic run through the sunset parking lot and back alleys had singed and seared its skin. Even though it was night, it felt like it was lying on an arid plain, underneath a burning sky.

It used to dream with the others. It would close its eyes and drift into a space of voices, the call-song of its kind. Its voice would join the others, dipping and looping and soaring. There was a strength and beauty to it, no matter how far apart they all were, they were joined. Yet as time went on there were fewer and fewer and voices, and the song grew desolate and sparse. Then it was just the creature, a sole voice in that wide empty space. It dreamed and sang alone. It knew it was the last of its kind.

It saw the boy climb from the window, a silhouette against the artificial light, and then drop down, landing awkwardly on the grass before standing up, gingerly testing legs and ankles. It pulled itself back into the shadows further, but the boy had stiffened, staring over, and started to approach.

Tom saw the creature pull back a little. He unwittingly took a step back himself and instantly felt annoyed, still thinking of the phantom camera that could be filming his every move, the future jeers of others if he turned tail and ran right now. It made a rasping sound, shifting again. One bony arm reached out, quivering as the noise came again. It sounded like it was saying '*water*.'

"Step aside."

Tom turned and saw a heavy-set man approaching him, around his father's age, in a faded green hunting jacket and wool hat. The man stepped past Tom, never taking his eyes off the creature. In his right hand, Tom saw that he carried a thick piece of sharpened wood.

"Go back to your house. Lock the door." He glanced back at Tom for a moment, but the boy hesitated, unsure if this was part of the prank, his adolescent pride keeping him in place.

"I said go home."

Tom shook his head. His friends were still out there, and he'd risked a lot sneaking out. This night was not over for him. The man muttered something, annoyed, but his focus was back on the creature which had pathetically started to crawl away, inch by terrible inch.

The man slowly walked behind it. He wasn't in a rush anymore.

He weighed the stake in his hand, the sense of anticipation growing. He wedged his foot under the creature's stomach and forced it to roll over. It lay on its back, looking up, an emaciated rib cage rising and falling.

The man approached, stake raised, and the creature made a desperate mewling sound and brought its spindly arms to its chest to protect itself.

"I think it's hurt," said Tom.

"Yes," said the man. "It's hurt."

"We should call someone. Get it some help." Tom wasn't sure if any of this was real or not, but his parents had taken him on a first aid course that summer, after his brother had had the accident at the local pool. Somehow this all felt connected, even if Tom couldn't explain why.

"There's a phone in the house," added Tom, unnecessarily, as if this might change things.

The man looked down at Tom again. For a moment he saw their positions reversed, another time, another place, when he was ten years old or so and his father had taken him out to the woods, where one of these creatures lay injured, leg caught in a double-spring bear trap. The man remembered the way the creature's mouth opened and closed silently, its wide eyes as his father handed him a wooden stake, nodded to the pale figure on the ground.

"Do it."

The man hadn't wanted to. He'd felt hollow, unsteady. He'd wanted to turn and run back through the trees, to the pick-up, to safety. His father had grabbed him roughly by the neck, forcing him forward. The request had become an order, then a shouted command. The stake didn't kill it on the first blow, or the second. The man had been led back to the truck, his t-shirt splattered with dark blood, his cheeks burning from tears. It had screamed and cried and even clutched onto his arms when the stake went in for the final time. His father clasped him on the shoulder. Told him he was a good son. He was proud.

The man told Tom to stay back and raised the stake again. He measured the angle, the creature below him. Yet he was hesitating, aware that his arm was still held aloft, like he was posing for a photo. He had spent most of his adult life hunting down these creatures, going from town to town, state to state, driven by some nameless fury that he had never wanted to examine closely. His father had given him this life and he had tried his best with it. All those years and it came down to this—

the final moment.

Still he stood there, his arm raised.

The boy was moving to stand in front of the creature. Like he meant to protect it. The man could easily push him out of the way. This could be over in seconds. All he had to do was act.

The excited laughter and chatter of children drifted by from neighboring streets. Soon they would wander home, high on excitement and sugar, back to houses, to warm beds, to families, to normality. Right now though, the suburbs were something else, something strange and unfamiliar, still full of ghosts and ghouls, vampires and werewolves, robots and aliens. And there were monsters too, lurking in the shadows.

There were always monsters out there in the dark.

Of the Hog Called Balthazar's McKay

John Sperry

1. The Swinedrovers' Offer

When the pannage of Pittsburgh was a legendary pig slop. More wilderness than city, the feeble settlement was treed enough to mast the entire Point. From the bulwarks at the Confluence east across the noxious marshes and up into the forests beyond Turner's Tomb, thousands of pigs were let loose to feed where they might: great black tuskers, wirehaired gruntlings, sounders of drop-eared Byfields. They gobbled up beechnuts and pignuts and acorns, and they grew fat and feral until they could be recaptured and driven north for slaughter.

Come first frost, the swine drovers descended from their mountain hovels and erected flimsy sties along the Allegheny's banks. From there they circulated an announcement, which was already known by everyone. They would pay out *one silver dollar* for each market-weight hog delivered to their care before the evening of the hunter's moon.

One silver dollar: good money.

Or rather it could have been good money, with the proper administration, but capturing an Allegheny hog is no small feat. The children of Pittsburgh formed hunting parties (the Braves of Wylie Street, the Cloven Knights, the Savage Company of Sounders), and they formalized pirate charters where shares of the silver dollar improved in accordance with age and rank and sex. Bonuses were awarded at standard pirate rates: one extra half-share for a broken rib, doubling of shares for impalement, quintupling for a lost eye. For those killed in the action: the allowance of two percent of all hog-related-income, in perpetuity, awarded to their mothers.

After the compensation of injuries, the lookouts were paid off and then ribboning bonuses were awarded for sticking a pig with company colors, because sometimes there wasn't the daylight to complete a hunt, and it was provocation to hunt another gang's pig. After all this, and a dozen other such instruments, so many hands had so many claims on the swine man's silver dollar, is it any wonder that most gangs chose to simply nail their prizes to the crown of a pin oak or else bury it in the dispassionate earth?

2. Nell Slingsby's Fraud

Nell Slingsby, the twelve-year-old commander of Nell's Nimrods, was desperate. Her Nimrods (all eleven of them) were a naturally dissembling lot and physically unimpressive. They haunted the spits of the Monongahela from Jail Street to the talus of Hanged Man's Bluff, avoiding the denser whorls of the eastern woods where market pigs made their burrows.

They'd paid for their timidity. Despite their name, the Nimrods had netted but a single hog in two years.

So, on the morning of the first frost, when a quorum of glum-faced Nimrods gathered near the nailors' stalls to discuss their season's dismal prospects, Nell delivered her proposal:

"What if," she asked, "we keep to hunting only 'tony pigs this year?"

The Nimrods chuckled, disbelieving.

"Come Nell," said Heth Billings, the youngest of the gang, "'*Tony pigs?* They're rubbish."

"Worthless!" Phinny Cowan chimed in. "No one'll pay for a 'tony."

It was true. There was one inescapable exception to the swine drover's generous offer: *they didn't pay shit for Anthony pigs.* Any pig (usually a runtling rescued from its own dam's laborious hunger) that thinks of itself as human, that shuns the fellowship of its own kind, that prefers, like the Nimrods, napping on porches to braving the wilderness, need not be hunted. The drover had but whistle, and the 'tony pigs came running, like trained dogs, to their own slaughter.

"Hear me out," said Nell. "We'll disguise our 'tony pig, and so—"

"Dress a piggy in your Mama's bed gown?"

The Nimrods laughed boisterously. Nell's face reddened.

"Mock," she continued, "but suppose that we lure a fat 'tony pig, a real tapster, raised on mash and milk, and we tickle her snout with spear grasses till her nostrils bleed, redden her eyeballs with snuff, and stick her with our colors. Next, we'll roughen ourselves: blacken our own eyes, lump our crowns, hmm? 'Twill then appear to any swine man that the Nimrodians have vanquished an honest vicious sow!"

This plan appealed very much to the Nimrods, and each was embarrassed to have lacked Nell's ingenuity. They vanished like smoke into the footways to see who amongst them could leash the fattest 'tony, except for Nell and Heth, who set out towards the marshes beneath Hogg's Pond, where sprays of spear grass might still be gathered.

3. A Beast Achieves the Point

But the mud beneath Hogg's Pond was deep and slick, a single odorous wet too difficult to navigate. Disheartened, Nell and Heth pushed south with only a bloom of crowfoot to show for their labor.

"Look," Nell whispered. She pushed Heth into the earth.

"Wha—!" he cried, but Nell covered his mouth.

She pointed to the river. Two hundred yards off, a massive shape, too large to be a beaver, was swimming across the Monongahela in their direction. At first, Nell supposed it was a black bear, bored with the spoils of Birmingham orchards, who swam to try his fortune in Pittsburgh proper. She couldn't recall a black bear ever visiting the Point.

She watched the creature navigate the Mon's shoals and sandbars with uncommon naturalness, like a ferry hand might, letting the current do the work when profitable. That was when she knew that it wasn't a bear at all, but a beast of greater intelligence. A hog, a boar certainly, so indefatigable he was unimpeded by the Three Rivers, which otherwise penned the pigs of Pittsburgh.

Reaching the shallows, the monstrous boar revealed himself: his pure white body the size of a wine butt, his fearsome black head with its Molossian brow and jowls. The boar's eyes were covered with fine lashes, like a mare's, and his four tusks gleamed like polished chalcedony. The beast shook the river from his coat and gave two terrible grunts, then marched towards the very willow thicket where Nell and Heth had made their covert. Too terrified to arouse the monster's curiosity, the pair held their breath.

The boar pushed his snout into the thicket and sniffed greedily. Nell could smell the pungency of his breath, the smells of soured cod and burnt black bread.

"He's Balthazar's," Heth whispered.

Nell bade him quiet.

"Who else, but *Balthazar's McKay*?"

The boar grunted once with satisfaction, then plashed away, eastward, into the forest.

"Nell! Nell! Leave him be!" Heth cried.

But Nell ignored him and followed the boar from a distance. Heth followed in turn. Nell did not know how long she was willing to pursue the hog, and she did not know what she would do if he stopped, but she understood that if Heth was correct, if the boar really was the hog called Balthazar's McKay, then she mustn't lose sight of him. After a quarter of an hour, they came to a stony place. The boar slowed his pace and stopped at last before an outcrop of fallen schist. He looked in Nell's direction, gave a handsome bow, then disappeared into a crevice in the stone-fall. She could no longer see the boar, but she could hear his intermittent squealing, which sounded for all the world like her own brother when he practiced Latin.

4. Possible Histories of Balthazar's McKay

The whole company of Nimrodians assembled before the outcrop. Except for tree patter, the place was silent. One brave Nimrod ventured to poke a stick into the crevice, but dropped it

when he heard an awful grunt. They'd circled the outcrop a dozen times over and confirmed what Nell had suspected: there was no second entrance to the den. The boar was truly trapped.

At last, Peter Prower spoke:

"Balthazar's McKay? You'll swear to't?"

"I will swear," Heth boasted, "there's never lived a larger hog."

"Looked right at us," Nell added. "Might've gored us!"

"Had he a black phiz?"

"Yes, and a pure white stomach and scimitars for tusks"

One of the Nimrods whistled lowly.

"Imagine what they'll pay for Balthazar's McKay…"

At this, the whole company erupted in speculation.

"We should seal him up, and fetch the drovers!"

"I've seen Balthazar's McKay myself, y'know."

"We should find a rifle."

"You did not."

"Did too! By Valentine's Ferry!"

"It's said come spring time, he wanders out to Indian country."

"The largest boar in America."

"Where'd we find a rifle?"

"Escaped from Balthazar's own singular."

"The Indians feed him venison, and he's attended to by a pair of virgins."

"He dances in their war dances."

"Fifty dollars?"

"He's no Indian! He's a ward of a witches' coven."

"The coven at Shelter Rock?"

"The same. 'Tis a demonic hog. A witch's hog!"

"The witches feed him snake flesh. They call him Centurion."

"He's descended from the same swine into which Our Lord cast the demon Legion."

"Blasphemer!"

"He'll gore us dead."

"Fifty silver dollars!"

"So," Nell said at last, trying to control her company, "what is to be done?"

"What if we seek Red Hector's assistance?" Heth asked. "He might concern himself with the boar."

The more Nell thought about Red Hector, the more she convinced herself that only he could secure their prize.

"Go and fetch him," she commanded.

But her Nimrods were uneasy with this alliance and wondered aloud how many of their shares an interloper might demand.

"Red Hector may have all my shares," Nell cried. "Now go and fetch him. He'll be at the parsonage."

5. Red Hector's Tale

On the subject of foundlings and their pedigree, people are inclined to one of two conclusions. Either the orphan's extraction is of some secret nobility (a bastard, a controversial heir), or else the vulgarest breeding. Red Hector Churchyard, with piebald locks and a cleft palette and a kyphotic spine, was agreed to be the latter sort of foundling. Red Hector's pallor was no redder than any honest yeoman's, his nature no less tame, but his crooked nose and especially his saint like sympathy with animals forever fixed the epithet.

Following a pair of Nimrods, Red Hector arrived at the outcrop like a withering dryad. He wore a patched over capote (scarlet once, russet now) down past his knees and no shoes at all. His spotted hair, matted with dead leaves and seedpods, was tied back with an eel skin.

Nell greeted this strange creature with a curtsy and giggled when he curtsied in return.

"Good evening, Red Hector. Our tale is not so difficult to understand. We've Balthazar's famous McKay holed up in this den, and we intend on delivering him to the swine sheds."

Red Hector said nothing but crouched on his haunches and stuck his face into the crevice. He inhaled deeply. Nell continued:

"I am prepared to offer you a tenth of whatever prize the hog commands, you understand? If only you'll fain to coax him gently from his den."

Red Hector made three sharp sneezes.

"'Tis a handsome offer," Nell added.

"Handsome offer, handsome lady! A tenth is a tithe. Handsome piggy, handsome prize!"

Nell glowered at her sniggering Nimrods.

"Might you coax him out, Red Hector?"

"Might I coax you first? Have you proof your pig is Balthazar's McKay?"

"Proof? He's the largest boar I've ever seen."

"Ah, you've seen many boars?"

"Well, he's a black head and a white rump. How many boars are thusly marked?"

"Ho, yes, marked. But is he black up to the withers? Are his forelimbs black in kind?"

Nell thought carefully before answering, "All his limbs were pure white."

"And of his ears?"

"Ears?"

"Pointy as a wolf? Droopy as a hound?"

"They dropped."

"Drops, ho! And of his curly piggy-tail?"

"Not curled, Red Hector, but straight and thick as an ox's."

"Very good, tithing lady. You've proven your prize. Your tithe. Neatly hemmed."

"You'll help us then? You'll get us Balthazar's McKay?"

At this, Red Hector went hysteric with laughter.

"Balthazar's McKay! Where is Balthazar's McKay?" he cried.

"In the den, of course!"

"Ha! This den? Balthazar's McKay was overran by a stage wagon two years past."

"A stage wagon?" Nell whispered.

"Two years past, on the turnpike. Split his belly into two. Sleeping, yes, but not in your den."

"Then *our* hog, Red Hector, the black head, the ears…"

"Those droops! No true McKay keeps droopy-ears, and Old Balthazar maintains no hog who's neither stagged nor barrowed. Your prize is a different hog, a greater hog than Balthazar's McKay."

"Who is he? Tell us, Red Hector."

"He calls himself *Ya'kwahewak*."

"Himself?"

"I'll tell you, tithing lady, the story of the Ya'kwahewak, and when I've told, you'll see yourself how dear your prize is valued.

"On midsummer's eve my story begins, ah, and I slumber in a fern bed. Beh-beh-beh! Beh-beh-beh! What sad bleating wakes me? Beh-beh-beh! I spy a pair of spotted fawns, as bedded in the ferns as I.

"A pair of fawns? No! I count. Two fawn heads. I count. Four fawn legs. I count-count-count, but cannot not find eight legs. Oh! I cry, You two heads, you share the legs. And so they do. Two heads. Four legs. Mother thinks she birthed a monster. Leaves you lost without her milk. We shall go to Doctor Hooker. To see how you might be fed. I'll call you 'Buck-Buck.'

"My Buck-Buck follows close behind me, gentle as the summer dew.

"But as we walk, I start to worry. Little Buck-Buck! Should I not name him, Buck-Bucks? Are they not two fawns, my Buck-Buck? Ah! I tickle Buck-Buck's belly. Four eyes close with satisfaction. Just one Buck-Buck. I scratch one ear. Do both heads receive the kindness? Who will say? When we rest, does one Buck-Buck dream of fresh clover and brother Buck-Buck ivy? They hear a noise, and Buck-Buck trembles. Both of them? Are they differently afraid? 'Tis the same fear! I try myself to dream like Buck-Buck, to keep two thoughts inside my head. Ivy. Clover. Clivy?

"So lost am I, in all these thoughts, I do not see what frightens Buck-Buck. The encampment! Oh, I am a fool. Men, two men, and a lady. A hut, a heavy lean-to, and a fire. I and Buck-Buck try to hide, but the men they are upon us. What's this? What's this? Are they delirious with drink? But no, it's true! A hunchback and a hydra. They laugh at me and at poor Buck-Buck. The lady says, I know a man back east, would pay a sultan's fortune for the fawn. Truly? Yes. Sultan's fortune. King's ransom. So, she shoots my Buck-Buck with her rifle. In the heart. The men both laugh. Do you think they died together? How many souls did I mislead?

"Too dark to see, I run away as fast as I am able.

"But I do not run so far. In buttonbush I hide and wait. They'll become so drunk and sleepy, I'll reclaim my Buck-Buck's body. They'll not be sold to men back east. I return to the encampment. The fire grows cold.

"Ho! Am I not alone? But I see another descending on the camp. A bear? A wolf? A pig! A boar. Outpacing me. He's on the camp, singing his war holler, and with his tusks he pulls down the lean-to. The earth shakes. The heavy logs fall upon the sleepers, mangles up their arms and legs. The beast kicks up the fire embers, smashes casks of hot spirits. Hellfire. The pitiless hog dances on the burning logs. They scream-scream-scream. He splits them with his whetter tusks. They stop their scream, and when the hellfire burns away, and the whole hollow smells of roasted meat, then the boar pulls out their bodies from the logs. I watch him eat from their bodies. He's a patient feeder.

"My name is Ya'kwahewak the Man-Eater," he tells me.

"Oh, I know not my name, though I'm called Red Hector Churchyard," says I.

And then Ya'kwahewak helps me bury Buck-Bucks' body, which isn't burnt at all. He digs the grave with his own trotters. Ya'kwahewak tells me the Buck-Bucks have forgiven me, both Buck-Bucks, two! And even today their grave is marked with a patch of wake-robin that keeps its flower all year round."

When Red Hector finished this recitation, the dumbstruck Nimrods watched him disappear into the den.

6. An Indecorous Toast is Interrupted

Kenhelm Ward was in a churlish mood. He was drinking with his fellow Bostonians-in-exile, who gathered weekly at the Whale & Monkey to gripe about the dismal slough called Pittsburgh. They'd fill their cups, then carp and cavil over the *putridity of their food* and the *malignancy of the weather* and, always, always, the *infernal tyranny of coal smoke.* Ward had supposed his time in Pittsburgh would be brief—no more than a fortnight! He was given assurances!—and now it had been seven months, and he had achieved no more than when he first arrived.

Ward had just proposed a toast, one which he thought very cutting:

"To the lasses of Pittsburgh, a sunny contrast to the stygian gloom of their native place!"

He'd prepared several more such lines, but the fellows at the table had ignored his toast; they were fixated on the windows of the tavern, on some commotion in the street, on the noises of some hellish circus coming from outside. The Whale & Monkey emptied itself in curiosity.

Outside, the chaos astounded Ward. At the top of street, a hog…a boar the size of a wagonette stomped and charged and squealed demonically. More confounding was the sight of the longhaired hunchback who, clinging to the boar's withers, rode the boar like a mule and shouted, "Ho! To the river! To the river, Ya'kwahewak!" This monstrous boar and his mad jockey were hounded by a gang of filthy urchins who showered the beast with stone missiles and screamed, "Our pig! Red Hector's stole our pig!" The drovers had lined the street, cracking their leather whips louder than pistol-shot, trying to slow the boar's advance, and they howled in the pig-gibberish of their trade:

"Whoo-ooo-eee!"

"Peeg-peeg-peeg!"

"Schweeeneee!"

The boar, incensed, spurred on by his infernal jockey, careened down the cart path, knocking over coal carts, toppling barrels of salted shad.

"To the river Ya'kwahewak!"

"Red Hector's stole our prize!"

"Peeeeeeeg!"

This whole nightmarish spectacle, thought Ward, unimaginable in Boston, seems suited to this backwards place.

One of the drovers nearest Ward had got hold of a long rifle, but his first shot went wide or else had no effect. The drover reloaded the rifle and took aim, but the boar was already upon him. The man cried out and collapsed, his thigh pierced.

"The river, Ya'kwahewak!"

"Red Hector's stole our pig!"

"Schweee-eeee-eeen!"

Ward gathered up the rifle and fired. The boar lurched then tumbled, crashing to the earth like a razed fortress. Hot blood stained his white belly.

Ward helped the drovers roll the great hog over, revealing the jockey's lifeless body.

"So," said Ward with feigned indifference, "Where do I claim my prize?"

One drover kicked at the boar's heavy scrotum and laughed.

"No prize for this boar! The hog inn't geld."

"What's that to do with it? He must weigh a half-ton."

"Tha' may be, but those balls, they taint his flesh and leave the meat foul-tasting."

"'Tis why we geld 'em when the pigs are young."

"Inn't no butcher'll pay for an entact boar. Uneatable."

"Not worth shit."

"Still," said Ward, lifting up the jockey's crumpled body by its hair, "I suppose someone still pays for dead Indians?"

"Yessir, that they will."

While white-armed Nell looked on and wept.

Brain Work

P. J. Schaefer

The man, Eldridge—or was he a boy, really?—sat in the old Bronco and stared at the green Range Rover two parking spaces in front of him. His focus rested on the rectangular window decal depicting a family: two large stick figures to represent mother and father, and three small figures to represent the children—one boy, one girl, and one baby of indeterminate gender. Adjacent to it hung a "Baby on Board" sign. Eldridge mumbled to himself. "No dog sign." Then he added, "I must be certain." He had to wait to make sure, but he had become well- practiced in patience.

Thirty minutes and two energy drinks later, Eldridge watched as the mother and daughter carried their shopping bags to the SUV, stepped into the vehicle, and started the engine. He waited until they pulled from the parking lot to the traffic light at the intersection with the main road before he started his own truck. "Now follow them," he muttered to himself. He expected they would not notice him; people rarely did when he was driving. Only when someone managed to glimpse his scarred forehead did people see him and then look away quickly. If he had had any understanding, he would have recognized the looks as those of pity or outright fear, but he lacked such comprehension.

After a ten-minute drive, he knew exactly where the family lived— at the end of a tree-lined cul-de-sac on a semi-private road—but he still needed to confirm the signs. He needed the baby. "I must wait and watch," he said aloud. He paused as if trying to remember something. "I cannot be seen," he reminded himself. He put his Bronco in gear and began to drive. "Neighbors are nosey. I must avoid them."

He found a safe, unobtrusive parking space two blocks away, just where the residentially-zoned area merged with the business area. "Park near a store," he told himself in that same, expressionless voice. As he started to close the Bronco's door, he hesitated. He started to reach for his tool bag, and then stopped. "Rushing makes a mess of things. Wait and watch first. Never act in daylight," he mumbled to himself as he pulled his hand back outside and closed the door.

Eldridge found a copse of trees and bushes to hide himself, and he observed the house for several hours. In all that time, no one entered or left the house. When he saw lots of neighbors coming back into the neighborhood, he remembered another idea. "I must return tomorrow," he whispered to himself. "In the morning people come out."

Twenty miles across town, a different family had left its home to rush to Cedars Memorial Hospital, where they sat in the Emergency Department waiting room. They had rushed there when their eight-month-old son, Michael had a sudden, violent seizure. They wanted him helped, wanted to know its cause and treatment, and hoped for a prognosis on the likelihood of such a seizure occurring again. Dr. Reese Lindsey stepped into the waiting room. "Mr. and Mrs. Mallack?" she asked as she walked toward them and took a seat facing them. "Your son has had a severe seizure. He lost consciousness and stopped breathing for too long." Dr. Lindsey paused briefly. "I'm sorry, but we could not bring him back. He is that 1.6 out of 1,000 who has died from the seizure, the so-called SUDEP."

Mr. and Mrs. Mallack remained silent for several minutes. "He died?" Mrs. Mallack asked. "No! No! That can't be!" she screamed. Tears streamed down her cheeks, and she stood abruptly. "No! I want to see him. He can't be dead!"

Dr. Lindsey had expected the response. She had prepared for it.

"Can we see him? Say goodbye?" Mr. Mallack asked quietly, as he held his sobbing wife to his chest.

Dr. Lindsey hesitated. "Are you sure you want to? Wouldn't you prefer your final image of your son to be more pleasant?"

Mrs. Mallack pulled away from her husband. "I want to see him!" she shouted, and so Dr. Lindsey led them to the room. But Michael no longer lay there. She had deliberately taken the child to one of the bio-hazard containment rooms with the claim that they had no idea what was causing the seizure. After she had called the time of death and angrily detached all of the monitoring machines' wires in a show of disgust that she could not save the baby, she had activated the switch that summoned the morgue people to fetch and cremate the body immediately to avoid the spread of contagious disease. Moving quickly

always mattered, and she knew Simon worked in the morgue that day.

"I am so sorry. They must have already taken him to the morgue," Dr. Lindsey commented as she led the Mallacks to the elevator. She knew they would not find Michael there, either, but she knew, too, that she had to act as if she expected to find the body there. After behaving as if she were shocked and angry at the discovery that Michael had already been disposed of, she left the Mallacks there crying over the loss of their child and the error made by the staff.

In reality, Simon, Eldridge's first mirror being had already crated and taken away baby Michael. Simon was driving the forty miles to Dr. Lindsey's private research lab in the woods, where Michael would join other babies. Michael had not actually died, but he did have the kind of malady Dr. Reese Lindsey wanted to use in her experiments. Like Eldridge and Simon, he would serve as an instrument of Dr. Lindsey's scientific passions. He might survive, and he might not, but he would definitely provide the brain matter Dr. Lindsey craved for her work.

Simon drove his van along the rutted road of the vast state forest until he reached the lab, a 2,400-square-foot, camouflage-green structure that held one room lined with cages, each one tall enough to fit a five-foot human, and many containing cribs instead of the beds some others held. Another room served as both a lab and a surgical theater, containing two lab tables; two operating tables; recording devices; and shelves full of test tubes, beakers, chemicals, closed and labeled containers full of brain samples, and a host of scalpels and other medical instruments. Another room, called the dark room, offered little more than a padded closet holding a chair, electrical equipment, and additional recording paraphernalia. The final room hosted a large incinerator and its venting tube.

As Simon brought the crate containing Michael into the holding room, he noticed Leroy, Eldridge's second mirror being, just locking one of the cages. Leroy had found his baby of the day by using the GoFundMe.com page Dr. Lindsey had shown him. He'd examined the posted images carefully and found the home and the baby. As Simon unpacked Michael, he noticed Leroy's baby's pink blanket. "A girl?" he asked. In general, Dr. Lindsey did not want baby girls. Leroy nodded. "Did what I was told," he said. Simon nodded back and closed the lock on Michael's cage. Then he and Leroy crossed the room to their own cages and lay on their own beds to sleep. Eldridge already snored in his own bed in another cage.

Morning found Eldridge back at the house on the cul-de-sac. First he watched the father drive off to work. Then the boy and his sister boarded a school bus. No dog came outside. At 9:30, the mother, carrying her baby in a combination multi-purpose carrier-car seat came out to the driveway. As she secured her infant in the car, her cell phone chirped, and she answered it. Eldridge could hear her side of the conversation. "No, I'm taking William to the pediatrician for his check-up, and then I'll be home for the rest of the day. Try me at noon."

Eldridge mused aloud, "William. That is a boy." He knew now what he had come to learn. "Midnight," he pronounced and started back toward his Bronco.

Eldridge returned to the lab, where he found Dr. Lindsey operating on baby Michael. He donned the lab coat Dr. Lindsey required and took his place with Simon and Leroy. All three stared, though none understood that the scars each one of them bore on his scalp, forehead, and ear area had come from a similar operation, each one a year apart, going back eighteen years. Dr. Lindsey could have used the ice pick method of lobotomy, but she preferred to go in through the skull after peeling back the scalp. She savored the scent and appearance of blood, liked the challenge of the surgery, and relished the stitching afterwards. Sometimes, she made patterns of the work, sometimes a straight line. Eldridge bore a straight line, while Simon had a zigzag pattern, and Leroy had a kind of chain pattern. Reese Lindsey's skill had increased over the years, especially for one certified not in surgery, but in general internal medicine. Her need, too, had increased; during the early years, one baby each year sufficed, whereas now she demanded several each month. After those first three years, her zeal had increased to the point that no baby other than the three standing before her had lived. What she called the "Early Boys"—Eldridge, Simon, and Leroy—had to incinerate all those bodies, just one of the many tasks which Dr. Lindsey had trained them to perform. She thought them useful but not really a success.

She focused on the brain before her, her goal to remove the piece she believed responsible for making the child male and the piece she believed made him epileptic. Then she wanted to insert the female brain part of Pink Baby into Michael's brain and Michael's male brain part into Pink Baby's brain. Eldridge suctioned blood, Simon held the receptacles for the brain parts, and Leroy worked on anesthetizing Pink Baby. The room filled with a cacophony of mantras.

"Hold it just close enough but not too close. Listen for the suction sound," Eldridge repeated steadily.

"Hands still so it doesn't drop. Stay in that exact spot," Simon chanted.

"Not too much but just enough. Look for pink skin," Leroy uttered.

Dr. Lindsey kept up her own monologue. "Let's see what we have here. It's this section right here," she announced as she plunged the scalpel into the particular lobe and sliced across it until it came free. She plopped it into the receptacle, and it slapped against the bottom. She turned then to Pink Baby, only her third ever female. "And now let us see what you have for me." She had just made her first cut into the scalp along the forehead when she heard the suddenly loud slurping of the vacuum tube behind her. "Eldridge!" she shouted, but she was too late; Eldridge had moved the tube too close to the brain, and the suction had pulled some of it right into the tube. Startled by Dr. Lindsey's yell, Eldridge dropped the tube entirely, and it flapped around the floor like a snake suddenly uncoiled. Reese Lindsey slammed down her scalpel and cuffed Eldridge on his right cheek. "Now I'll have to wait until you bring me the next one," she shouted as she watched Michael's breathing stop. "Fire this one, then clean up and go. Now!"

His face still stinging, Eldridge lifted baby Michael and carried him away. Simon and Leroy stood frozen in position, awaiting their orders. "Put it in the first empty jar, Simon," Dr. Lindsey said and then turned to Leroy. "Clean up the blood, and put her back in the crib. Then clean my instruments." Reese Lindsey stomped away then, unbuttoning and throwing her lab coat to the floor as she moved. She slammed the door and traveled outside to her car. She drove away quickly, dirt spitting out from under the car's tires.

Ten minutes later, Eldridge started his truck and drove to the cul-de-sac. The home lay in darkness, though he was two hours earlier than he had planned. "Midnight is best," he muttered, and then corrected himself. "Always do what Doctor says." He left the truck and checked the property and house for signs of alarms, just as Dr. Lindsey had taught him. "Clear now. A-okay," he told himself. He moved to the French doors on the back deck. Then he pulled his glasscutter from his tool bag and used it to make a hole in the glass pane, so he could reach in, grab the doorknob, and open the door. "Now find baby," he whispered to himself. Practice had taught him he needed to go upstairs. This house, though, stood out as different. Usually, he went to homes with only one baby. He did not understand the ways that one change would affect his search. He had simply known he had to get a baby quickly or get sent to the dark room. But Eldridge had been trained to move silently, and he used that skill as he searched the house. He had much greater control of his body than he had of what remained of his brain. He found all four bedroom doors open, each room bearing the small beams offered by a night light. He needed only to look into each one from the hallway to find the one he needed. Finally, in the last room on the upstairs hallway, he saw the crib. He moved quickly to it. He reached into his tool bag for the rag and ether. "Only a little and not too much," he told himself, and then covered the baby's mouth and nose with the wet rag. "Keep you quiet," he muttered to the baby. Then he lifted the infant from the crib and walked quickly to the doorway. In the hallway, he stood still for a moment, uncertain which way to go. Then he saw the stairs and headed toward them. Just as he reached them, the boy came out of his room. He started yelling, and Eldridge panicked. He stumbled down the stairs at a run and smashed through the glass doorway without even opening it. Glass shards clung to him and the baby, but he kept running, up the street and around the corner, once again in his panic, uncertain about where he needed to go. The baby's father now followed him, shouting, "Stop! Bring our baby back!"

Eldridge kept running, blood streaming down his face and arms. Finally, he reached the right area and dove into the Bronco. He did not bother to put the baby in the waiting crate; he placed him on the back seat, started the truck, and screeched off. "Just go home. Just go home. Just go home," he kept muttering to himself.

Eldridge heard the sirens, but he did not know they were for him. He could not see any cars behind him; he looked only ahead to his pathway home. When he saw the road he needed, he turned onto it and finally slowed. After he reached the lab and parked, he opened the back door of his truck and saw that the baby had rolled onto the floor. He, too, bled from his face. Eldridge lifted him. "Just bring baby inside," he told himself, and he carried the baby forward.

When at last Eldridge laid the baby in an empty crib inside one of the cages, he wiped his own face clean and started brushing the glass away. Only then did he hear the pounding on the outside door. "This is the police! Open the door!"

Simon and Leroy had awakened at the sound, and they moved to stand next to Eldridge. They stared at the door. Not one of them knew what to do.

The police decided for them. They used a battering ram and burst into the room. Initially, they did not know what they were looking at, but then the images registered: cages holding babies, three badly scarred men or boys, and doors to other rooms that might hold additional horrors.

They moved toward the boys and slipped the handcuffs on them easily, though each one wailed in his own way, the sound of frightened, injured, and confused animals. "Doctor! Doctor! Doctor!" they kept repeating.

"Doctor?" the police officers asked in unison, incredulous that a doctor might have created such a place. "We'll find that doctor," they said, but they never did. The boys had called her only "Doctor"; they knew no other name. They did not have enough vocabulary to describe her. No one believed the doctor was a girl; everyone assumed the boys were confused. The lab existed in the woods, on a huge parcel of state land: no permits, no ownership, no anything to trace. The video evidence showed only the procedure, the boys, and a small pair of hands—no face. Except for the two newest babies, none of the others offered any clues, for their remains had vanished in the incinerator. Dr. Lindsey escaped detection. Yet, every time a baby goes missing, the police officers wonder if the boys' "Doctor" has resurfaced....

Roser and the Guide to the Inexplicable

Samantha Pilecki

Kenny Roser. Red-headed, sweaty-faced, Kenny Roser. He grew up on Fadden Street in a brown and beige split-level house, went to school where he had no friends (except the lunch aides). Overheated, pathetic, Kenny.

But then he found the *Guide to the Inexplicable*. It was a guide to the abandoned, the unsettling, the distinctly odd history of his otherwise coddled surroundings. And Kenny found who he truly was: Roser, a researcher, explorer and archaeologist of sorts. The *Guide* gave him something to be a *part of*.

The *Guide* was published bimonthly on pulpy-feeling paper, somehow dustier and more unpolished than any magazine Roser had ever held. It had a feel like fur; it had a feel like skin. Like history and a multitude of lives already lived.

Because of the *Guide* (and his newly acquired driver's license), Roser had found the blood-stained pews of Tenant Church where Revolutionary War soldiers had bled and died. He'd seen the graffiti on the tomb-like walls of seven-foot high sewers; he had heard the disturbing dialogue of the dead, drugged and disconnected, on the tape recorder he left at the abandoned Bellevuille asylum.

All this, all by himself.

Roser picked up the newest issue of the *Guide* from his truck's passenger seat and tucked it into his backpack where a flashlight, an extra pair of socks, a water bottle, and the tape recorder were. *Guide* expeditions were just that: expeditions. And he wasn't taking any chances with Ridge Valley.

Roser stepped out onto the clipped grass and shut the truck's door, the sound swallowed by the line of trees surrounding the massive lake.

Roser considered the blank sky above; no stars, no moon. He was alone, again. Of course. He'd never been part of a 'we,' ever. He'd been just Kenny. Apart.

He crossed the grassy expanse, stopping at the sandy edge of the lake. Ridge Valley Reservoir was quiet the way only nature could be: a whirring of insects, the *shushh* of the lake. Roser appreciated the glassy obsidian of two thousand acres of water laid out in front of him. Each place in the *Guide* was captivating, but Ridge Valley uniquely so. The valley had been flooded. On purpose.

Like everything else the *Guide* covered, Ridge Valley was a man-made monster. It was flooded during the 40s to provide a city reservoir of drinking water in case something went terribly wrong during the war. But a stubborn trio of farmers, an old couple with their imbecile son (imbecile being the term the historic record showed), flat out refused to leave and were annihilated during the scheduled flood.

Tragic yes, but *Guide* material? Not until '62, when the three Burnes brothers capsized their fishing boat. Then there was a submerged town *and* six bodies somewhere in those two thousand acres of water.

Again, not yet *Guide* material…but legends had to start somewhere. One of the Burnes brothers resurfaced in 1978; and that summer Jakub Ravagio's and Marcus Miller's canoe overturned in front of witnesses on a calm day. Marcus they saved, but Jakub was never found.

One up, one down. Six bodies.

In '82, a couple of amateur divers found another Burnes brother, the skeleton still wearing boots and the remains of a fishing vest. A week later, Richard LaMeyer committed suicide in Ridge Valley and his body resettled somewhere in that ghost village at the bottom of the lake.

Always six down there. The reason the *Guide* mentioned Ridge Valley now was because a fisherman hooked a human foot out of the lake. Whose, they didn't know, but even this needed to be avenged, Roser knew. There needed to be balance.

Roser inhaled, smelling a day of roasted sunscreen and pine needles reduced to its inverse self, like the negative of an image. Haunted, like a nightmare.

He wondered what it was like down there. The shadowed, aquatic growth, the preserved tin mailboxes and fences and farming equipment. The water was freezing in April, even at the surface; falling in was likened to having a ghostly glove grip you, seizing your muscles. And down you'd go. Because once the wind caught your boat the right way, once it capsized and you hit the ice-cold water…

You were done.

A voice? Or just a fluke of nature? Roser turned on the tape recorder. *Six*, he thought, standing at the edge of the lake, boot heels in the sand and toes in the water. *Six is your number.*

The water was soaking through the toes of his boots. It wasn't bad. Just cold.

Six is our number.

Not a fluke. Roser stood, edging the toes of his boots further into the water. The tape recorder buzzed in his backpack. Bugs screeched in alien unison. Roser took another step, the water soaking through into his socks.

He waited. Alone. Alien, himself. And then the smell of his grandmother's coconut frosted cake came at him, swift as if an oven door opened.

Thoughts of her linoleum floored pantry, stacked with canned fruits and crackers. Of lazy afternoons watching old cartoons on her mint rug, *that cake* baking in the kitchen just around the hall.

What do you want from me? he thought.

More.

Of course. The answer wasn't heard this time, so much as felt.

What's it like? Roser thought. *What's it like down there?*

The bugs kicked up from the trees, their enormous drone in answer.

We are powerful, the language of the bugs says. *We are massive. Give us more.*

We. How potent, to be a *we*. Roser contemplated the changing expanse of water around him, its oil-dark surface flattening and flaring in witchy rhythm. There was more inside Roser, more *they* wanted to turn over in their hungry mouths. So, he gave it to them, immersing himself in memory, drifting on the wealth of his life. The time when he was ten and discovered a wild raspberry patch while riding his bike, the fruit made all the sweeter by his physical suffering. (Even at ten, little Roser wasn't inclined to exert himself, but the berries were surely the world's way of making it up to him.)

Or a song—he could give them a song, the only one that could touch him lately. It came on the radio all the time last year, when he rode the bus home from school. Those words eloquently echoed his exact misery, and then told him it'd be okay.

Or the movie theater. Not that he'd see a movie by himself. That would be too painful. He could imagine the looks, the nudges, the pity from people. But no one could stop him from getting a popcorn, with gloopy, golden yellow butter. And the concession girl would be there. Even though her skin was bad and she was just as big as Roser, she always smiled.

Whispers rose in the air around him, floating off the trees in distorted bug song. They were pleased. These were the things the dead missed; these were things he could give them.

But he could give them more…

Of course they wanted more. More memories, more life. And although he didn't have much else, *life* was indeed something he could give them…

Roser edged his feet further into the lake.

No. Not you. Not yet.

Roser, as if awakened from a trance, stepped back out of the lake, tripping over his feeling-robbed feet.

But will there be somebody else? he wonders.

Yes. And then, what Roser waited to hear, no matter where the *Guide* led him. *Will you come again? We would like that.*

We.

"Of course," Roser said out loud.

The wheels on his recorder rolled on. Proof that he was not alone.

The Wedding Gift

Christopher Calix

Tracy Beck was not wearing her best formal dress to the wedding. Her best formal dress, a lovely blue silk number, was hanging in her closet encased in a cocoon of plastic wrap. It would hang in her closet until Rebecca Whitmore's wedding in the spring. That would be a *real* wedding. Today she was wearing a dress she wouldn't even consider a runner-up to the blue dress. It was a pale pink dress that had been to so many events in the ten years she had owned it that it was starting to fade and the hem was loose in a spot on the skirt. She hadn't selected this dress despite these signs of wear but rather because of them. In fact, when she had dug it out of her closet she had planned on throwing it away. But no, she had thought, no. This would be the perfect dress to wear to the wedding of little Jenny Beck and Kris Abdallah.

She looked over at her husband who was driving with a look that openly displayed the anger and spite she had been feeling upon waking that morning. The night before had been quite different. Tracy had been in such shock she couldn't even look at him. She had lain on her side, facing away from him, staring into the wallpaper long after he had turned out the light and gone to sleep. It had been the one time that Jimmy Beck had ever raised his voice at his wife, the very first time he had stood up to her.

The shock and surprise that had silenced Tracy so efficiently the night before changed instantly to anger and resentment the minute they woke that morning. Jimmy had turned to her and given her his usual sleepy approximation of a kiss on the cheek but she remained as immobile as marble. She was thinking of the night before and the things he had said.

She honestly hadn't thought it was going to be a big deal, surely not the big blowout fight it had quickly turned into. They had received the invitation five months prior. It had been with dread that she plucked the pretty silver envelope from the pile of mail upon seeing the return address label. She had half a mind to bury it in the waste can under a layer of Burger King coupons right then. Jimmy had come into the kitchen just as she had opened it.

"Awww," he had said, reading over her shoulder. "About damn time."

"Well, you can mark yourself as a party of one because I shall not be attending," she had told him.

She had told him. That was what had caused her surprise at his wrath the night before. She had told him!

Had he not noticed her shake her head when she caught him marking the date on their Norman Rockwell calendar? Had he failed to notice her complete lack of preparation for the day, the dearth of any wedding presents?

So, when he had asked her what time they should depart the next morning, his response to her stern reply of, "I told you, I am not going," was completely unexpected.

His face turned the crimson color of a ripe cherry. She had seen him get red in the face before but then it had been when she had commented at the sight of his round pink belly peeking out from the bottom of his t-shirt or when she had laughingly told him in front of a table of his co-workers that his fly was down upon his return from the restroom.

But this was not like those times. This was not her bashful, embarrassed Jimmy. The man before her, this red-faced angry man, was a stranger. He was as foreign as the furious voice bellowing from his chubby depths.

"Goddamn it, Tracy! We are going! You are coming with me! This is family, for Christ's sake! My little sister!"

She tried to reply but found her throat had tightened in upon itself in shock. She swallowed before mumbling, "But Jimmy, those people…"

"Damn it, Tracy!" he yelled, jabbing a finger at her. The finger came perilously close to striking her in the chest and she backed away, sinking into the sofa behind her. "I don't give a flying fuck what your political beliefs are. You're gonna get over your prejudices for one damn day, you hear me!"

She nodded silently and kept nodding until he was out of the room. When he was gone she stayed sitting on the sofa, her mouth agape and her eyes unfocused.

He may have been able to shock her into submission last night but Tracy would be damned if she was going to be a happy witness to these nuptials. She had not spoken a word the entire morning and now, looking at Jimmy driving with his dumb, placid smile, singing along to John Fogerty and getting half the words wrong, she realized that he hadn't even noticed. The anger within her burned that much brighter; she could imagine her subpar pink dress being singed by the heat of her wrath. She turned away from her husband and looked out the window.

Jenny Beck was not a pretty girl. At least not pretty enough to justify how foolish she was. Tracy had always thought her a fool. Aside from Jimmy's occasional mention of one of her short-lived stints in community college or the odd appearance at a family dinner, Tracy's sister-in-law remained on the periphery of her life.

But for Tracy the moment she became involved with Kris Abdallah was the moment that Jenny had graduated from mere fool to pure idiot.

Tracy couldn't fathom it. How could she have allowed herself to be drawn into that lifestyle? With those people? How could she debase herself to such a disgusting degree? Those people were responsible for nearly all the recent death and destruction around the world. They were sick, perverse. It was shameful. She felt a rolling wave of revulsion, as thick as pudding, course through her body just thinking about it. With a quivering hand she pushed down the button to lower the passenger window and allowed the cool wind to hit her face until her stomach had settled.

Once revived, she closed the window and directed her attention back to her oblivious dullard of a husband who was now bumbling the lyrics to Creedence Clear Water Revival. She glared at him and with a relish hit the tuning button on the radio, effectively stopping "Fortunate Son" in its tracks and settling on a Trisha Yearwood song. Jimmy just smiled, as docile and content as an infant.

He might have slid the scale of power in his favor last night but no more. She would stay no more than thirty minutes into the reception and not a fraction of a second more. She wouldn't even *look* at the cake. Just enough time to drop off the present and—

"Jimmy! We didn't get them a present!"

The abrupt sound and loud volume of his wife's voice, absent all morning, made Jimmy jump. He looked at her as if finally noticing that she was in the car with him.

"They'll get their gift. Don't you worry about a thing."

She looked at him as if he was the simplest fool on God's green

earth, which in fact she did and planned on telling him so immediately following the wedding. Hell, maybe during. What did she care if those two got a gift anyways? The only thing those two had coming to them was a one-way trip to the bowels of H-E-L-L. Now she was mad at herself for having ceased her silent treatment. She crossed her arms and glowered out at the passing scenery.

They were about thirty miles outside of town now. They passed fruit stands and straggly fields with rows of cattle. It was overcast but somehow still bright, the sun unwilling to be diminished by the sprawl of grayish clouds. Finally, their arrival at an area slightly more civilized was heralded by the appearance of a Circle K and rows of fast food chains on either side. They turned off the highway and drove on to the main road of a newly sprouted suburb with "Now Leasing" signs posted outside of each stuccoed housing development.

Jimmy turned into one of the new housing complexes. This one featured a blooming cluster of pink and white balloons posted to its leasing sign. Tracy watched them sway in the breeze and realized with grim acceptance that they had reached the wedding site. They had been invited to Jenny and Kris's newly purchased home three months prior. Mercifully, Jimmy had gone without her. If only she had been so lucky this time…

Jimmy parked in one of the aisles that lined each side of the street. As the engine died down and the music turned off Tracy thought that her husband of seventeen years would offer some small condolence or a thank you, anything to compensate for the abject dread she felt.

But he merely tightened his lips into what could have possibly been considered a smile and said, "Okay, let's do this."

Usually Jimmy was a gentleman and solicitous towards his wife to the point of annoyance. She would often bat his hand away when he tried to take hers when crossing the street or when he attempted to place it along the small of her back. Today he was walking ahead of her without even glancing back. Tracy purposely slowed her gait, loitering behind him in an attempt to get his attention. She knew she was behaving like a child and she didn't care. She would have liked to throw herself on one of the driveways and pound and kick at the asphalt in a truly spectacular tantrum. But Jimmy kept walking on ahead and she quickly ran to catch up.

Tracy saw with distaste that there were even more of the pink and white balloons outside the house. How tacky, she thought, unconsciously shaking her head.

They followed a middle-aged couple into the house. They were obviously on the bride's side. The man held the wedding gift as she adjusted her wrap; a sharp contrast to her own husband who had screamed at her to come to this wedding and who had then run away from her once they'd arrived. She glared at the back of his head as they stepped inside.

A petite blond in a short purple dress greeted them and gave them each a small bag of rice tied with ribbon. "To toss at the happy couple!" she winked at them, as if the whole thing was an inside-joke between just them three.

They walked through a spacious living room and into a hallway. The guest bathroom was on the left and to the right was a study where she saw the couple that had been in front of them set down their gift amongst a whole bevy of brightly wrapped boxes. She wished she were setting down a gift too. It could've been anything, a box of dung, a fruitcake, anything so that her arms weren't empty. She felt like a freak coming to a wedding without a gift. But then she realized she was at a wedding with real freaks and, for the first time that day, Tracy smiled.

Through the kitchen she could see the backyard where rows of white plastic chairs faced a makeshift awning. Most people were already seated. It was obvious which side belonged to the bride's party. Rows of seats alternating with suits and dresses, combed hair and coiffed curls. And on the other side…the groom's party.

Suddenly Jimmy's pulled her aside by the arm. "Will you get that grimace off your goddamn face?" he seethed in her ear.

To her credit, Tracy hadn't known she was grimacing. She had merely been thinking that she could smell the groom's party, that their stench had wafted over to her through the open glass doors. She had been wondering if their kind ever bathed.

She tried to shake his arm off but his grip tightened. "Listen to me. You leave your politics at the door. For just one day you are going to be tolerant and accepting and you're going to congratulate my baby sister and her new husband with a big goddamn smile on your face. Do you hear me?"

He pulled her roughly by the arm and they found their seats in the back row.

Again, she was afraid of the man she had married. The same man she had to scold for farting in public. The same man who would snore until she punched him awake at night. This same man was now swearing at her and pulling her around like a sack of trash.

They sat in silence waiting for the ceremony. Tracy wondered what kind of ceremony it would be. Would it be in English? Would there be some kind of sacrifice? What would the groom wear?

And then from a stereo seated on a stool to their left, the bridal march began to play. She watched as the wedding party paraded to the front, one couple at a time. The bridesmaids wore dresses in a shade of light lavender. Tracy tried to avoid looking at the groomsmen entirely.

And then like a cobra being drawn out of its basket by a bagpipe, the bride arrived. Jenny looked ecstatic. How she could be that happy when she could plainly see just WHAT was waiting for her at the end of the aisle was beyond Tracy's comprehension. Her dress was simple and not elegant simple but *cheap* simple. Her hair was pulled back in a twist and she clutched a bouquet of daisies tied with a long pink ribbon.

Had it been any other wedding ceremony in the world Tracy would have brought her "wedding hanky," a worn handkerchief gifted to her by her Great-Aunt Pearl. She would have had to press the soft fabric at her leaky eyes to save her mascara. But during these nuptials Tracy's eyes remained bone-dry.

The actual ceremony closely followed every other wedding ceremony she had attended and was thankfully brief. The only moment of discomfort came at the end when the couple kissed and Tracy had to hide her face in her hands. With the couple officially wed and promenading back down the aisle Tracy was that much closer to fleeing this house and never returning.

People started rising from their chairs and mingling with one another while a handful of sweaty teenagers began stacking the chairs and bringing out large folding tables. Tracy stayed seated, watching them spread tablecloths over the tables before a group of ladies began carrying serving platters and bowls and setting them down on top.

She got up as the teens started clearing the row of chairs in front of her. Jimmy had gone off somewhere without her noticing. Now standing she felt awkward and unsure. Leaning against the wall, she tried to make each vertebra make contact with the white stucco, as if she could be absorbed by the building and disappear. From inside, she could hear catcalls and people congratulating the newlyweds. Two of the groomsmen sauntered past holding red plastic cups, the smell of beer trailed behind. She didn't know they drank beer....

Tracy's breath caught in her chest as she saw someone striding purposefully towards her, two plastic cups in hand. She made a move to angle herself away, so that her body language would clearly state *stay away*. But as the woman in the yellow dress drew closer Tracy saw that it was Cheryl Connors.

"Honey, you should not be empty-handed today!" Cheryl said, handing her a cup.

"Oh, Cheryl! Thank God you're here!"

Cheryl was Jimmy and Jenny's aunt by marriage and thus seemed as outside of the day's events as she was. Tracy didn't think she had ever felt so happy to see another human in her life.

"Are you kidding? I wouldn't have missed *this* for the world!"

Tracy rolled her eyes. "At least we'll have some stories to tell afterwards, right?"

"Oh. Well, yes. I also got some great pictures of the ceremony!"

"Hopefully, you didn't get any of the groom's side in them. Makes me sick just looking at them," Tracy replied, taking a sip from her beer. "I mean, I get it, it's legal and all now. But that doesn't make it right! You know we had one move a block away from us? Disgusting. These freaks are always trying to rub it in our faces! And now we have one in the family. I'm just sick over it."

When Tracy had finished and taken a large gulp from her beer she saw that Cheryl was white in the face. She looked as if she had just witnessed Tracy kicking a puppy.

"Excuse me," Cheryl said before turning, her mouth puckered tighter than a drunk's hand around a highball.

Tracy watched as she walked away. Apparently, she was the only sane, normal one there. People were coming back outside, assembling in little clusters and crossing the lawn to the food tables. She felt very alone again and suddenly her spot against the wall didn't seem so safe. From across the patio she saw that Cheryl was now speaking to Jimmy. When she saw Cheryl gesture towards her and Jimmy's angry scowl, Tracy launched from her spot on the wall and went inside through the open glass doors.

She ducked into the kitchen. There were only a few stragglers as most of the party had followed the food. There were groups of pre-filled cups of beer and Tracy ditched her empty cup for one filled to the top with white froth. She drained it in hungry gulps and wiped the foam from her mouth with the back of her hand.

"Someone sure was thirsty!"

Tracy started at the sound of the man's voice. Her eyes trailed up his suit to a face that could only be described as- actually, Tracy was hard-pressed to find any words to describe what she was looking at. He was obviously on the groom's side.

Her face must have registered her total horror. "Sorry, didn't mean to frighten you." He was holding a plate of ribs. She looked down at the sauce-laden bones and felt her stomach lurch forward as if it too wanted to escape the scene unfolding.

"So, are you a friend of little Jenny?"

Tracy was mute. Unable to look away she watched as he took a rib and sank his teeth down on its ruddy flesh. Her silence was broken by the tiny terrified whimper she emitted when she saw him pull the rib away from his mouth. They both stared at the rib, held in mid-air between them.

Attached to the rib was the lower part of the man's jaw.

He shook the rib once and his jaw fell to the counter. Unable to turn her gaze elsewhere, like someone was physically pushing her head downwards, she looked at where his jaw had landed. The skin was sallow and had the thin and dry consistency of an onion peel. There were a few gaps in the row of teeth. Two of the teeth had fallen free when the jaw had landed; she supposed the others were still embedded in the rib. There was, of course, not a drop of blood.

With a third of his face missing, the man tried to speak but it came out as a guttural, indecipherable grunt.

Tracy screamed when she looked up at his face. Strands of dead flesh dangled from his cheeks. Somehow, his tongue was still attached to him and it dangled obscenely, a thick slab of meaty gray flesh undulating in the air. It wriggled lamely in its effort to speak and she screamed again.

The few left in the kitchen turned and looked at her with disgust. *At her.* Not at the cadaver with part of his face missing, but at her!

When she tried to flee from the man and his missing jaw, he grabbed her arm, not unkindly, and he looked at her apologetically, again attempting to speak. She shook herself free and ran out of the kitchen and into the hall. The tears started falling immediately, flowing freely and rapidly down her face. The sounds of beer-fueled laughter and conversation carried from the backyard. She wanted to find Jimmy and she wanted to go home. Where was he?

With a shaking hand she wiped at her damp face. Her hand came away with a smear of black mascara. She realized she had ended up crying at the wedding after all. The beer in her otherwise empty stomach provided her with just enough gumption to walk back outside and search for her husband.

Walking back past the kitchen she didn't turn away fast enough and saw several guests attempting to ease the man's jaw back into his head. She shuddered heartily and walked faster.

The sun was setting outside. Tracy didn't want to be here when it was dark. Standing on the patio she sought her husband's normal, human face, which for once would be a welcome sight. Pacing the patio and searching desperately amongst the wedding revelers, she felt just as she had when she was six years old and had gotten separated from her mother at the grocery store.

While pacing she stepped on something and heard a foreign crunching sound. Looking down and expecting to see a snail or a bug she jumped a foot backwards upon finding a human finger. It had likely belonged to a woman, one who favored red nail polish. The red colored nail looked bloody and obscene next to the jaundiced skin. Tracy retched twice and ran back into the house, colliding against one, and then two, wedding guests.

That was it; she was done. She would go outside and stand by the car until this nightmare was over. Screw Jimmy; he could come out and find her himself. How quickly her revulsion turned into rage at the mere thought of her husband. How dare he bring her here! How dare he think it her wifely duty to party with— She couldn't even think of what you were supposed to call them these days. The life-impaired? The living challenged? Well, screw being politically correct. They were goddamn zombies is what they were. Goddamn flesh-eating zombies! If Jenny wanted to marry into a pack of these creatures that was her own tough luck but Tracy was not having any more of this. One could only take so many errant body parts.

Trying to walk rapidly without drawing any attention to herself, she went back into the house and dashed down the hallway. She had just reached the front door when someone moved in front of her, blocking her escape. She gave a tortured moan before seeing that it was Jimmy.

"Jimmy, you take me home. You take me home now."

"What the hell are you doing? Running around the damn house, screaming. You are embarrassing me." He spit out each word like it was a source of vileness that needed to be removed from his mouth at once.

Again, people were staring at her. They were coming in from the kitchen and living room to peer at the woman with mascara dripping down her face get scolded by her husband. She tried to keep her voice down. "I am embarrassing *you*? How dare you, Jimmy. How dare you bring me here, how dare you leave me with all these—these—zombies!"

At the utterance of the Z-word a loud collective gasp rang out amongst their audience. People shook their heads, disgusted by her and her slur, her and her now naked hatred.

"Please take me home, Jimmy! Take me home!" She buried her head into his shoulder, leaving a trail of Maybelline Lash Spectacular mascara on his lapel. She hadn't been this vulnerable in front of her husband since their wedding night.

He patted her back gently. "Let me just say my goodbyes," he told her in a hollow, defeated voice.

He turned her back around and guided her back through the living room and down the hall. She allowed herself to be pulled along and she cried into her open hands. He gave a quick nod to someone. When she looked up she saw that they were nearing the backyard and she started to struggle and squirm away from Jimmy's arms.

"Shhhh. Just wait in here. I'll be back in five minutes," he told her quietly and gently pushed her into the study. She nodded duly and he closed the door.

Tracy took a deep breath and wiped her face with the skirt of her dress. It was dim in the room and she flicked the lights on. All the presents in their festive wrapping, boxes both big and small, were heaped on the floor and on the desk. Absently, she wondered where the couple had registered.

Only a few minutes had passed before the door opened again. There was Jimmy. But he wasn't alone. She recognized the groom and two of his groomsmen. They entered the room one at a time except for Jimmy. Without looking at her Jimmy closed the door, leaving her alone with the groom and his undead friends. One of them pushed the lock in the doorknob and the small click she heard made Tracy go cold all over.

"Well, what are you waiting for, Kris? Enjoy your present!"

Their eyes which, she realized in the light, burned and shone like the blue part of a flame, burrowed down on her.

"No, no…" Tracy pleaded, backing away.

Kris was first. He dove down on her and buried his teeth into the soft flab of her upper arm. The other two followed. The pain exploded all over her as if it was all she had ever known. But despite the pain, despite the soft mewing sounds falling from her drooling mouth, she was able to stay conscious. She was able to stay standing and conscious right up until she heard the little popping noise her socket made when the groom ripped her arm from her body. It was the last sound she would ever hear.

The house was silent. After the events of the day the absence of noise was like a comforting presence in itself. Kris Abdallah was at the sink, washing his face. He had to be very gentle for fear of ripping skin or accidentally removing his nose. The newly anointed Mrs. Jenny Abdallah came up behind him, wrapping her arms around his waist and resting her face against his back.

She exhaled a happy contented sigh.

"I love you," she said, her lips rubbing against the fabric of his t-shirt.

"And I love you," he replied as he gently patted his face dry with a washcloth.

"Oh," he said as if just remembering. "Please thank your brother for the thoughtful wedding gift."

The Receding Dark

Dwayne Martine

No one knows how it began. Some say it was destined. Others point to an Apache woman from New Mexico who knew what to do. Others still say something was loosed that day the first protector was assaulted, something from the very earth, some memory unburdened and set free.

But no matter how it began, the movement was undeniable. They came from everywhere. They emerged from red rock caves, from carved out arroyos, from the hollows long ago built under cemeteries, from deep forest dwellings and from abandoned stone ruins. They came from office buildings, churches, cities, bordertowns and the deepest parts of every reservation. They were all drawn to this river and the camp of thousands here.

A line had been drawn months ago. Ordinary folks who grew tired, dropped what they were doing and placed themselves in the way of an oil pipeline being laid in sacred land. These people prayed, sang and danced in the hopes minds would be changed, that this latest act of outrage would cease.

They burned herbs, cedar, and sweet grass. They prayed through the day and the night for their various deities from over five hundred different tribal Nations to come to their aid. White Buffalo Calf Woman was prayed to. Changing Woman was prayed to. Water Helper Katchinas were prayed to. And yes, Jesus and the Blessed Virgin were also prayed to. And all to stop this most recent desecration from taking place.

They rode horses, set up tipis, camps, schools, kitchens. All people of many Nations gathered to protect the water of which we all are made. They gathered in the home territory of the Lakota of Standing Rock.

This is an old story, as old as this country, these continents. A force from outside coming to tear the people away from the lands that they called sacred. And so, it was that this latest outside force brought guns, batons, armored vehicles and a force of hundreds to move these people and continue the work of empire.

Two lines drawn in the earth. And the people would not be moved. They held their ground, never fighting, never backing down, always praying and singing and remembering what was most important: the living earth, their mother, all our mother.

So, the outside forces beat, cajoled, shot, mocked and terrorized the people. They bruised, broke, handcuffed, and arrested these who would not be moved.

And maybe it was that first fist slamming into the body of a water protector that word was loosed and the others called. Maybe there was a person who was not man nor woman, who watched the television, phone or computer and thought that this was what generations had been preparing.

This person gathered the night and sent out crows, coyotes, owls, text messages, rats, black beetles, worms, social media posts, blue-tailed lizards and poisonous snakes to others who would be receptive to this dark Word.

These who received the Word laughed, spit, crossed themselves or started to turn the message back. They would not be moved.

These others were the dark end of centuries of knowledge passed down generation to generation, from ancient times, from before the great migrations up from worlds before. These were the purveyors of sorcery, of magic, of the inverse of medicine.

And they were selfish, object-oriented, hateful, ambitious and could not see past themselves the purpose of helping any other without enacting a cost, most often asking for the very lives they craved destroyed, which gave them power.

They were bank executives, homeless vagrants, childless women, angry men. And then there were those who were neither man nor woman, who gathered the greatest power, who hurt themselves over and over, who cut at their spirits until there was almost nothing left holding them together, to garner the energies needed to perform their tasks.

They preyed on their own. They cursed rival clans, families. They sent death to strangers who might have just bumped into them in a crowd or said some slight others would have let go. And these who would not be moved took pleasure in the pain wrought against the water protectors by the outside forces of hate and violence.

Then whoever sent word to these doubled down on their gambit.

These dark agents were told once the violent forces overtook the water protectors the violent ones would come for them.

"Once every inch of land is taken, they will hunt you down, they will complete the destruction started centuries ago. No one will remember you. You will not be mourned. And your story will end there. There will be no more destruction for anyone."

And the world would watch, bemoan some abstract loss, take minor note, and move on. Then these dark agents looked at their hands, took notice of the ruins in which they lived, counted the number of dead for which they were responsible, made note of which stars pointed to which structures on the land, and noticed which way the wind went. They looked for signs.

And one by one, they lifted their heads from bowls of blood, from images of ash, from pictures bitten into bark, from moving shadows refracted from clear crystals, from computer screens, from cliff carvings which predicted this day and they moved.

So, they came. From all corners of two continents they gathered.

Just before the dawn this morning, an old woman clad in a long, simple red dress and covered in a black shawl appeared down the road. She moved but no one could remember seeing her walk. She was just there.

And the water protectors were all woken by those who had been protesting all night. They whispered. And the whisper spread among each other and soon they left, they ran, they crossed the river on foot, crushed body into body into vehicles while in motion and rode on their spooked horses over the rise.

The outsiders, in their armor and black boots, from their military vehicles and regimented lines roared and cheered. They exhaled and took off their helmets. They smiled. This battle, if not the war, had been won, they determined. They broke their line and began to settle into the centuries old slouch of self-satisfaction and entitlement passed down to them.

But as the first vehicle started and began to leave, human forms were seen gathering again across from them.

More dirty fucking Indians, they thought, re-donning their helmets

and armor, pulling dogs that whined and cried and tried to pull away from their masters. They re-made the line.

These new protesters seemed to appear from nowhere, out of impenetrable dark headlights, portable lights and flashlights could not break. Many were dressed in black. None of them carried flashlights or lanterns, except for a few torches burning low and the three dozen or so lights of cell phone screens.

There were a handful, then dozens, then hundreds extending far back into that unbroken night. There was no moon.

It is as if all sound, the wind, insects, vehicle hums, human speech had all been taken and only the space of their absence was left and felt like still water all around.

Then it started.

Women began singing, bone whistles pealed through the quiet, drums started with strange two-thirds beats. Many were laughing.

They pulled bags of dusts and powders from their clothing. Knives were revealed. Necklaces of beads were removed and pulled apart with force. Canes and staffs with crow and owl feathers were raised. Human skulls were placed upside down in the dirt. Long reeds were raised and pointed.

A woman, whose face was lineless but whose hands were gnarled like wood knots reached under her dress and pulled out a handful of her own pubic hair and lit it, throwing it to the ground. She motioned the black smoke before her, mouthing whispers that could be heard from a distance. She cut her left hand and let blood drop into the fire. Her eyes were not eyes but hollow sockets that stare as if seeing.

A man fell to all fours and the buckskin cape covering him seemed to flatten to the ground. The cape is not a cape. It is the white skin of a mountain lion turned inside out. The head lowered, revealing eyeholes staring straight ahead, black and empty. When it raised, yellow blinking eyes shown.

The man's crouch turned into a full, fluid, feline arch, with only his human hands and feet turned to impossible angles beneath him. Many like this man appeared: coyotes, wolves, elk, bulls, and many, many black dogs. Even from the air and slithering from the earth came crows, owls, snakes, frogs, lizards and pests.

Many who were well dressed in suits and tasteful dresses simply looked at their cell phone screens or iPads and moved a finger of their left hand over the surface. From these simple motions, stories, chants and songs would be played back on their devices.

Until now the armored outsiders had been silent, staring, shaking their heads, smiling and disbelieving the night and its tricks. They nudged each other and told one another that these tricks were fooling no one, that this latest act of cowardice would be avenged.

Two lines were drawn. On one side, the darkness writhed. On the other, the outsiders laughed and shook ready their mace cans.

No one knows how it began. Some say it was an Apache woman from New Mexico who knew what to do first. Some say it was someone from a northern tribe. Some more say it was definitely a beautiful Hidatsa woman. Still others say it was a stranger, who was neither man nor woman, who first crossed the line.

A rattlesnake wrapped around an officer's foot. He thought about his wife and two kids just before the venom hit his heart. He fell.

A large owl flew from nowhere and reached into a blonde woman's helmet, gouging out her eyes, tearing off her nose and opening her cheeks. She had just enough jaw left to speak one word: Jesus.

The wolves and mountain lions which were not wolves or mountain lions lunged at incredible distances, tearing through the bullet proof armor and opening chests. Beads made from bone and precious stones taken from the jewelry of the dead were shot with reeds, rifles and human femurs at the officers, always finding a weak spot in the armor. The pain was instant and excruciating.

A gray mist from the dark crowd moved over the officers, leaving bodies with limbs turned at impossible angles. Others raised skull-shaped whistles to their mouths and released the sound of a thousand men screaming in pain. Still others cut their own bodies and inserted objects that then appeared under the skin of the officers.

From the margins of this dark crowd came nude runners, wearing blue and black masks of upside down faces, running at inhuman speeds. They grabbed the officers, never stopping or slowing, pushing aside cars and armored vehicles and then they sped off to where the dark was thickest.

An old Navajo woman, who folded her legs under her, sat. She wore simple clothes and a satin headscarf. She had a stick which she used to draw in the earth. If you looked closely you could have seen tears stream down her face. She looked like someone you once knew. She motioned with her left hand, palm up to the officers. They stilled, as their clothes were torn off their bodies, as then their flayed skin flew into the now starless night.

The officers no longer laughing, no longer stunned, raised their rifles and found they did not work. Their vehicles shut down. The sound projector stopped. Their cell phones and cameras went dark.

They moved hand to hand, encumbered by armor. The dark ones moved around them easily, slitting throats, cutting off the whorls of the fingertips, toes, penis and the top of the head.

A short lean, dark brown man with a simple line of feathers on his head and down his back raised a club with thin black mirror like edges embedded in the length. He ran at an officer and brought the weapon down, tearing the man in half. He continued running and, like he was sinking into quicksand, lowered completely from sight until gone.

There was blood everywhere. The black dogs and coyotes which were not dogs nor coyotes lapped at it to get their fill.

In the dark, eyes closed as the terror mounted and the voices of the attacked officers were heard screaming in these others' heads. Then as suddenly as it began, it stopped. These others stepped back from the spectacle. They all moved as one. Besides the first few lines of torn and broken officers, the dozens behind them stopped their flight and turned around as one also.

She was beautiful, perfect from every angle. Long lithe limbs walked, graceful and measured, out of the darkness. She wore a simple blue dress. She was barefoot. She seemed to glide over the bloodied earth. She smiled and the world fell away. She seemed to mouth words that the sound coming from her mouth did not match. There was a momentary pause, a confusion as she spoke. But what she spoke was as clear as if she were speaking into your ear.

"I am called by no name and I am called by every name. I live within the light and the source of the dark. I have been called here this night to undo the darkness of my relatives. I have been called here after months of prayer to undo what has been done."

"Look and your wounds are healed. Look and your bodies are whole. Look and the darkness has receded. Look and these, my relatives, are gone. The darkness will not win out today."

As she said this, the dawn appeared over the eastern edge and, with each beam of light spilling over the horizon, the gathered dark people disappeared. The other line of people looked and their bodies were healed, their vehicles worked and the world around them did not shift or pull them into its unknown folds. They were whole. And the woman spoke again.

"I am the moon when it is full and I am the sun when it is dark with eclipse. I am known by every name that has been prayed for here these months. I am the peace that has been prayed for come from the dawn."

"Look and the water protectors will leave in peace. Look and they return home because I am here now. Because of this you have no purpose here. You may return to your homes as well."

The gathered officers watched as the protesters appeared from over the horizon, gathered their camps and began to leave.

No one knows how it ended. Some say it was a white officer from Ohio. Some say it was a black man from Michigan. Still others say it was a blonde woman from Bismarck who crossed the line and began shooting.

The woman was first hit in the arm, then the leg, then the rest of her body as she fell backward. Though she could, she did not protect herself. They did not stop. She rose from her prone position in the dirt and sat with her legs under her as they continued to shoot. She raised her arms as bullets struck and blasted past her. She held a feather in both her hands and lowered her head. All the officers heard what she said then as if she were speaking into each of their ears.

"And even this we shall forgive."

She then stilled as the sun fully rose over the horizon and the officers cheered.

Dressage for Beginners

M.P. Diederich

After dinner, Colonel Bainbridge suggested that we retire to his study to enjoy a few snifters of brandy along with the Cuban cigars Lt. Pferder had been so thoughtful to bring along. Considering the Colonel's advanced age and ill health, I would normally have advised against such indulgences, but I held my tongue in light of the festive nature of the evening. Had I spoken up, the Colonel most likely would have twisted his whiskers and advised me to save my professional medical opinions for my patients, my being a veterinarian and all.

"Yes, yes, I know it's a bore to you young, vigorous lads to hear me droning on and on about the glories of my own youth," said the Colonel, filling three glasses on the sideboard. "Please, please sit down. You can just shove those papers aside there, Pferder."

"Pardon my curiosity, sir," said Lt. Pferder, examining some of the pages on the sofa, "but what are all these charts and diagrams? More work on Wellington's gambits at Waterloo?"

"No, no, not at all," said the Colonel, handing each of us a glass of brandy. "Just a hobby of mine, one that the inexorable advance of age has consigned to an unrequited passion in my autumn years. You are, of course, familiar with dressage?"

"You mean training horses to dance around and the like?" asked Pferder.

"Dance? Hmpfh!" the Colonel snorted, holding the cigar box open to me. "Nonsense. That's how our modern age views the noble equine beast, I'm afraid. Just a curiosity, obsolete in this world of motor cars and aeroplanes—the hobby of doddering old men like myself. No, my good Lt. Pferder, the art of dressage is a far nobler pursuit than that."

"I beg your pardon, sir," said Pferder. "I assure you I meant no offence."

"Of course not. Please, please take one of these fine cigars you were so kind to bring with you. I can't just hoard them all to myself. At my age I can't have such sumptuous temptations around. Let me get that lit up for you and, *voila*! Now, shall we toast to someone's health? Mine is beyond even the purview of the Almighty, I'm afraid."

"To Old Vic, then," I said. "That old scamp just might outlive you yet."

"Old Vic?" asked Pferder, incredulous. "Surely you must be joking."

"Not at all," said the Colonel. "Dr. Featherstone here is quite the veterinary physician. He may be right about Old Vic after all."

"But a horse," said Pferder, taking a puff on his cigar, "surely can't live that long. He must be damned near sixty by now."

"Fifty-seven last week, if you can believe it," I said. "Still as fit as ever, though he's slowed a few paces, naturally."

"Yes," said the Colonel, "I once read of a horse reaching a full sixty-one years of age. I suppose Old Vic has a few years left to achieve true distinction."

"I'd say he's quite remarkable as he is, sir," said Pferder. "To Old Vic, gentlemen."

"Not so fast, my boy," said the Colonel, his tone lowered and far graver. "Let us not forget the reason for our gathering this evening: the bitter anniversary which unites us three old guardians of His Majesty's Empire."

"My dear sir, I am truly sorry and must beg your pardon. I didn't mean to forget—"

"Oh, none of that now," said the Colonel, his broad, reddened face twisting in an attempt to mask his emotion. "We all know full well that you of all three of us carry my son's death heaviest on your heart."

"Sir, there was nothing to be done. John, you were there—you saw what happened, what we were up against!"

"Yes, yes," said the Colonel, dismissing Pferder's protests with a wave of his immense, tanned hands. "John and I both know all about it. Those bloody Boers and their ambushes. Wouldn't fight like honourable men, no. Half-Dutch, half-savage if you ask me. No, my boy, if it I who must beg *your* pardon. War is a terrible thing. It's not all that romance and rhyme in the Valley of Death. Please, you must forgive me. It dishonours Herbert's memory to lay any blame at your feet. Come now—let's celebrate, for who knows what the morrow brings?"

With that, the Colonel's spirits rose considerably, carrying us on to a second and third pouring of liqueur and another round of cigars for all.

"I must say, my boys," the Colonel laughed, "it does this old warhorse good to see the Empire passed down to such young men of good heart—

present company excluded."

"And a bloody shame of a wreck you lot left it, old man," I laughed.

"Hear, hear! That is a good one, my boy!"

We toasted again, generally of proud and festive feelings in good company. It was Pferder who seemed a bit distant, gazing again at the stack of papers on the leather sofa.

"Please, Colonel, if I may ask," he said, "could you explain this fascination with dressage, of all things?"

"Ah yes, it does seem a bit incongruous for an old officer of the Fifth Dragoons to spend his dotage mucking about with show horses. But you know well my love for the beasts, or shall I have you tour the stables again, maybe offer a dram to Old Vic?"

"Well, of course I understand the horses, sir," said Pferder. "We're all of us old veterans of the Fifth, after all. I just wonder what it is about the particular pursuit of dressage that so intrigues you."

"Surely, surely," said the Colonel, straightening himself as if preparing to deliver one of his lectures at Sandhurst. "You see, for me it is the epitome of love, dedication, and respect for the intelligence and majesty of the equine species to commit to the perfection of a single horse in both physical and mental fitness so as to become one—bonded, if you will, to the noble beast as if to a brother-in-arms. After all, you're not just teaching a horse to parade along the ground, but to march as if before the King himself in full review. It isn't far removed from moulding some raw recruit into the very paragon of a modern soldier."

"That's quite…moving, sir," said Pferder, a bit gobsmacked. "I never knew you were so committed to this art."

"Oh yes—I'm writing a book on the subject. Just a slim little volume. Dr Featherstone here has been kind enough to assist with the anatomical and zoological information."

"Really, John? I didn't know you were more than a sawbones for the four-legged," Pferder laughed.

"Purely mercenary work," I assured him with a smile. "The Colonel is underwriting my whole practice out here. Personally, I'm just glad to have the occasional sojourn from the hoof-and-mouths and breached calvings."

"You know, I did always wonder what you buggers were up to out in the moors. I guess it can't all be gloaming and pining for Heathcliff. So, when shall I expect to see this opus of yours in print? I'd love to reserve a copy."

"Of course, of course," said the Colonel. "It's all but finished, although you are sitting on some of the galleys there."

"Oh dear! I beg your pardon," said Pferder.

"Here—let me freshen your drink," I said.

"Cheers," said he, looking over the proofs. "'*Dressage for Beginners.*' Oh, well that is quite a charming title! I'm very much looking forward to it."

"I wouldn't pin your hopes on that," I said, handing him a full glass.

"Oh?" said Pferder quizzically. "Is something the matter?"

"Please, please sit," said the Colonel. "Oh, don't look so dramatic, Pferder. It's nothing to do with the book. It's just, well, I've not been entirely honest about my concern with dressage, nor my interest in horses in general."

"Oh no? Well, please tell me, sir; I'm dying to know."

"Yes, yes, I bet you are, my boy," said the Colonel, pouring himself another brandy and slowly pacing about. "Well, well; where to begin? I suppose back at the beginning, when I was but a young man, just twenty-two and full of ambition and vigour. It was 1854 and I'd just received my commission as a lieutenant in the Fifth Dragoons, just before we set off to fight the Russians, of all things. Help the Turks take the Crimea, who even remembers why? It didn't matter much to me, of course. I just wanted to leave England, see the world, see the fear and respect one could command standing tall in bright, Imperial reds. Oh, we were all fools in those days.

"Of course, you must know about Balaclava, the Thin Red Line and the Charge of the Light Brigade and all that? Even in defeat we tend to make a grand tableau of it all. All I saw was death, smoke, and misery. Broken bodies of men trodden under hoof. Whole squadrons blasted to bits by the roar of the howitzers. Tennyson never wrote of the way a horse's legs still twitch while the blood spurts out from the stump where its head was lately perched."

"I'm sorry, sir, but I didn't realize," gaped Pferder in awe. "You were in the Charge? The six hundred?"

"Damn it, Pferder," the Colonel bellowed. "Don't you know a damned bloody thing?!"

"That was the *Light* Brigade, Jim," I whispered to Pferder.

"The hell is the matter with you? Bloody lieutenant in the Fifth Dragoons and you don't know the bloody difference between light and heavy cavalry?!"

"I…uh…"

"It's all right, Colonel," I said. "Lt. Pferder's just a little hazy on his military history."

"I should say so," said the Colonel. "Well, that was the same bloody mistake Lord Raglan made, you know—sent the wrong damned brigade charging in. It should've been us. But it doesn't bloody matter, of course. Fifty-four bloody years ago—just last week was the anniversary, if you can believe it. And now nine years since my Herbert breathed his last. Don't get old, gentlemen—that's a bloody order. Now, where was I?

"Oh yes—the whole damned battle was a bloody melee even before the Charge. The Russians ran headlong at the 93rd and were cut to pieces. Then we were sent to counterattack. Somehow in the smoke and fog I was separated from my platoon, and then my horse was shot out from under me by a mortar blast—sent me flying ten yards through the air. By the time I came to it was dusk. The valley was a desolate waste, littered with the hideous, mangled bodies of shattered men and the bloated hulks of the dead horses. All of my kit was still attached to my horse—a beautiful chestnut colt he was, bred right here in Yorkshire by yours truly. I'd bought him as a foal from an Italian chap and trained him myself. It broke my heart to search amongst the carnage for poor Vincenzo—that was the name the Italian stable man had given him— but I didn't know what else to do, standing alone and hurt in that horrid, smoky twilight."

"How dreadful," said Pferder. "Did you ever make it back to your platoon?"

"Yes, yes, eventually, but not before I came across a sight which in all my long years will never fade from my vision. There I was, half-mad with thirst and desperation, when ahead of me the smoke parted like a curtain to reveal the silhouette of a great, majestic horse, standing still, its head bowed down to the ground. At first I thought I must be hallucinating, but no, it was him: Vincenzo, somehow revived, though with blood streaming down his chest, which was torn through to the muscle and sinew from the mortar blast. And then I saw, to my utter bafflement and horror, that Vincenzo was eating the corpse of a fallen Russian soldier."

"Oh balderdash!" Pferder exclaimed. "I must say, sir, you had me on for a moment there. That is a good one. Ha! To think, John, that we'd sit here and believe that a bloody horse could rise from the dead, and to feast on the flesh of a dead man to boot! My word, Colonel Bainbridge—if it weren't for the influence of your fine brandy and all, I'd say you'd gone utterly mad. That is just too much."

"Well, you see, Lieutenant," said the Colonel, continuing on calmly and with less gravity, "at first I thought that the Russian was dead. It was only when I drew nearer that I saw his feeble attempts to push Vincenzo away."

"Colonel, please," said Pferder, "that is quite enough." Pferder stood, placing his empty glass on the end table. "If you will not desist in spinning these wild and depraved yarns, I shall be forced to bid you good evening."

"Please, Lieutenant—I beg of you to sit down."

Now standing behind Pferder, I placed a hand on either of his shoulders and gently pushed him back down onto the sofa.

"What's all this then?" he asked.

"Now, now," said the Colonel. "I apologise for the vivid manner of my description, but, you see, I was quite terrified, watching the beautiful colt I'd raised from a foal devour the entrails of that helpless, screaming man. You must understand, then, that I cannot help but relive the experience."

"John," said Pferder, putting a hand to his temple; "could you fetch me some tonic? I feel a bit lightheaded."

"And you must further understand," the Colonel continued, "that I realized in that moment that I would have to subdue this hellish beast one way or another, either through sheer brute force or through the determined strength of will."

"John, I feel very faint," said Pferder. "I fear that I'm really not well."

"So, you see, Lt. Pferder, my keen interest in the proper subjugation of my horse in a rigid, rigorous manner. And you may further understand that I do not suffer flippant fools who shirk their duties in the face of the enemy, who disobey the orders of their commander under fire, jeopardizing the whole operation to save their own skin."

"John…John, are you there? I can't see!"

"When Herbert gave you orders, you should have followed them, trooper," said the Colonel. "At ease, Lieutenant."

"John…I…" Pferder tried to stand at this, but his limbs gave out from under him, and he collapsed to the floor.

"All right, John," said the Colonel. "Let's both pray that you gave him the proper dosage. Even Pferder here doesn't deserve to wake up after Old Vic starts in on him."

I nodded, and together we lifted poor Lt. Pferder off the carpet, each of us praying that we wouldn't have to see Old Vic begin his midnight feeding.

Contributors

Charlotte Byrne graduated with an MA in Creative Writing in 2016. Her short story "Soldiers All" can be found in *Tales of the World* (2013, DualBooks), and her two flash pieces "Sardines" and "Not Tonight" are published in *Purple Lights* (2016, Fincham Press). Her humorous piece "Stuck" appears on the *Funny In Five Hundred* website. When not fussing over manuscripts, she can be found swearing like a navvy, guzzling tea, or cuddling dogs—often simultaneously.

Christopher Calix's debut novel, *Dead Celebrities*, was published in 2016 by Lethe Press. He received his MA in Literature from San Francisco State University.

M.P. Diederich was born somewhere in New England in 1985. He studied English and Creative Writing at Fordham University while seriously considering joining the French Foreign Legion. He currently lives in Brooklyn with his wife and two small panthers.

Casey Ellis graduated from Manhattanville College in 2004, where he wrote a senior thesis on ethical issues in Oscar Wilde's *The Picture of Dorian Gray*. He received a Masters in English from the University at Buffalo in 2006, with a thesis on the language of the fool characters in Shakespeare's major tragedies. Casey was the editor of *Startling Sci-Fi: New Tales of the Beyond*, and line editor of *Southern Gothic: New Tales of the South*, *Behind the Yellow Wallpaper: New Tales of Madness*, and *Salon Style: Fiction, Poetry & Art* which featured his short story "The Creature from the Lake." He is currently an adjunct professor of English.

Daniel Gooding was born in 1984. His short story "Crow Magnum Xix" is featured in the *Startling Sci-Fi: New Tales of the Beyond* anthology published by New Lit Salon Press, and he has also written for *The Guardian* website. He lives in Bath, United Kingdom with his wife and two children.

Andrew L. Huerta lives in Tucson, Arizona where he teaches technical writing and is looking to publish a collection of short stories entitled *A Different Man*, and his first novel, *Raggedy Anthony*. His short stories have appeared in such publications as *Chelsea Station Magazine*, *The Round Up Writer's Zine: Pride Edition*, *Creating Iris*, *Jonathan*, *The Storyteller*, and the anthology *Queerly Loving*. His personal essay, "Divorce and Evolution: A Case Study of a 'Joto'" is included in the anthology, *Fashionably Late: Gay, Bi, and Trans Men Who Came Out Later in Life*. For more information please visit: www.andrewlhuerta.com.

Oliver Ledesma is a 28-year-old living in NY who likes fantasy, horror, and weird fiction. In his spare time, he likes to read, write amateur short stories, and apparently dress up like a satyr.

Jack Lothian works as a screenwriter for film and television and is currently show-runner on the HBO / Cinemax series *Strike Back*. He has had work published in *Helios Magazine Quarterly* and the anthologies *Triangulation: Appetites* and *Down With the Fallen*, as well as a graphic novel *Tomorrow* alongside the artist Garry Mac.

Dwayne Martine is a poet and writer living in Scottsdale, Arizona. He has been published in national and regional print and online journals, including *Kweli*, *Malpais Review*, *Yellow Medicine Review* and others. He has an undergraduate degree in English from Stanford University. He works as a professional technical writer in the financial services industry.

Samantha Pilecki works as a librarian and therefore has typical librarian interests, namely caring for rats, collecting dead bugs, and smoking cigars. Her work has appeared in *El Portal*, *The Fable Online*, *A Prick of the Spindle*, *Typehouse*, and other literary magazines.

P.J. Schaefer's work has appeared in *Troika, Dogsongs, Elements, Ink., Poor Katie's Almanac, Behind the Yellow Wallpaper: New Tales of Madness, Salon Style: Fiction, Poetry & Art, A.T.Q.: 19th Century American Literature and Culture, The Facts on File Companion to the American Short Story, The Facts on File Companion to the American Novel,* and *Kate Chopin in Context.*

John Sperry is a writer and printmaker from Pittsburgh.

Luke Spooner a.k.a. 'Carrion House' and 'Hoodwink House,' currently lives and works in the South of England. Having graduated from the University of Portsmouth with a first-class degree he is now a full time illustrator and writer for just about any project that peaks his interest. Despite regular forays into children's books and fairy tales, for which he has won awards for literary and artistic merit, his true love is anything macabre, melancholy or dark in nature and essence. He believes that the job of putting someone else's words into a visual form, to accompany and support their text, is a massive responsibility as well as being something he truly treasures. Visit Luke at http://www.carrionhouse.com/.

Sarah K. Stephens is a developmental psychologist and a senior lecturer at Penn State University. Although Fall and Spring find her in the classroom, she remains a writer year-round. Her short stories and essays have appeared in *LitHub, The Millions, National Book Critics Circle: Critical Mass, Five on the Fifth, The Indianola Review,* and *(parenthetical).* Her debut novel, *A Flash of Red,* was released in December 2016 by Pandamoon Publishing.

Ken Teutsch is a writer and performer living in central Arkansas.

Michael J.P. Whitmer is a father, husband, and speculative fiction writer, casting a shadow in his sunny hometown of Jacksonville Beach, FL. Find him tweeting @MJPWhit.

The NEW Series

For generations, genre fiction and literary fiction have been perceived as irreconcilable. With the NEW series, NLSP strives to prove otherwise. NEW is an ongoing series of illustrated anthologies that highlight the literary merits of different genres and styles often looked down upon, forgotten, or not taken too seriously in the literary community. The first three books in the series, *Southern Gothic*, *Behind the Yellow Wallpaper*, and *Startling Sci-Fi* explore *NEW Tales of the South*, *Madness*, and the *Beyond*, respectively. With over 50 authors and counting, NEW features some of the best writers working in genre fiction today. Many go on to publish novels and win awards. All the stories in the NEW series are complemented by original artwork created specifically for each story by a singular artist per title.

Also available from NLSP

Southern Gothic:
New Tales of the South
edited by Brian Centrone
and Jordan M. Scoggins

Behind the Yellow Wallpaper:
New Tales of Madness
edited by Rose Yndigoyen

Startling Sci-Fi:
New Tales of the Beyond
edited by Casey Ellis

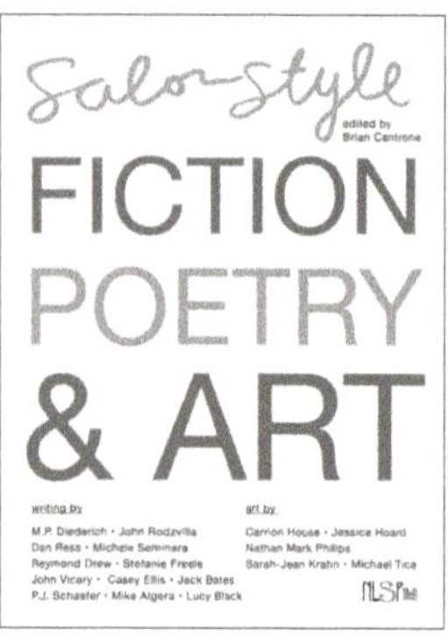

Salon Style: Fiction,
Poetry & Art
edited by Brian Centrone

I Voted for Biddy
Schumacher:
Mismatched Tales from the
Mind of Brian Centrone

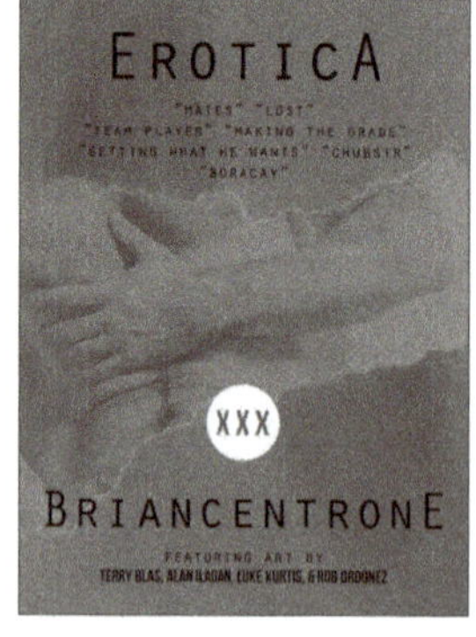

Erotica
by Brian Centrone

For more information visit

www.newlitsalonpress.com

www.ingramcontent.com/pod-product-compliance
Lightning Source LLC
Chambersburg PA
CBHW061125100726
47911CB00013B/683